# TAKING ON WATER

# DAVID RAWDING

*Taking on Water*
Copyright © 2014 by David Rawding. All rights reserved.
First Print Edition: July 2015

ISBN-13: 978-1-940215-55-6
ISBN-10: 1940215552

Red Adept Publishing, LLC
104 Bugenfield Court
Garner, NC 27529
http://RedAdeptPublishing.com/

Cover and Formatting: Streetlight Graphics

*I dedicate this novel to my loving and supportive parents. I know how lucky I am, and I'll never take that for granted. Thanks for working your asses off, Mom and Dad, so I could sit on my ass and write this book. Also, I'm sorry for cussing.*

# PROLOGUE

WITH EVERY PULL OF THE rope, Tucker Flynn brought the trap that much closer to the surface. He lifted the lime-green lobster trap out of the water and slid it down with the other two on the trawl. His cracked hand pulled the throttle lever to a standing position, putting the *Periwinkle* into neutral. He worked through all three traps quickly, separating the lobsters that were too short from the keepers. After slipping bands over the keepers' claws and dropping them into the live well, he restuffed the black mesh bait bags until they bulged with frozen mackerel chunks. When the last bait bag was cinched tight, he closed the trap doors with a clatter of the plastic-coated wires.

He put the boat into gear and scanned the water. Better to lay the traps in the shallow, rockier places that other boats didn't dare traverse. He turned the wheel sharp, banged a U-ey, then slid the traps off in his wake so they would land parallel to shore. The season was finally producing. Tucker eyed the well holding the six keepers he'd gotten from the last set as his boat slowly trolled along the coast.

When he rounded the bend, he noticed another lobster boat bobbing amid a clutch of motley-colored buoys. Two suntanned deckhands in canvas white V-neck T-shirts and tight-fitting jeans milled about Tom Braxton's deck. Braxton had been in the lobstering business since Tucker's father's day and was known to be ornery as a bull kicked in the junk.

As he guided the *Periwinkle* closer to his buoys, Tucker wondered if he would morph into Tom in another twenty years

1

or so. A subtle wind brushed his cheek, and he spied suspicious gray clouds rolling up from the southeast. Tucker cruised by Braxton's boat, whose name — the *Water Angel* — was painted in black, sloppy letters at the stern. The *Water Angel* probably had five feet on Tucker's boat and a few more in girth.

One of Braxton's deckhands gave Tucker a deadpan glare. The man, holding a curved filet knife, leaned against the boat rail with his legs crossed as if he were loitering outside a convenience store. His brown eyes and dark features were part of a black-stubbled thin face and accompanied by a mustache with combed whiskers. Without breaking Tucker's stare, the man moved his lips, saying something that made his companion, who'd been leaning over the boat's side, spin around. This guy had a similar face but a thicker frame, his body and shoulders resembling a boat mast and his chest puffed out like a sail.

Movement in the *Water Angel's* wheelhouse drew Tucker's eyes away from the men on deck. He saw Braxton, a guy who resembled a walrus more than a man, especially in his orange fisherman's bib.

Braxton and his new two-man crew didn't acknowledge Tucker as he circled their boat to locate his traps. Tucker plucked a blue-and-white buoy out of the water and almost fell over backward when he found no resistance. The line had been cut. He let the painted chunk of Styrofoam and plastic clatter across the *Periwinkle's* deck.

"I hope this is some kind of coincidence," he muttered. The fact that the buoy hadn't yet drifted away was a clear sign that it wasn't though. His hackles rose like tiny spikes.

Tucker spotted the other buoy he'd left in this cove as it floated around the bow of the *Water Angel*. He could tell that it was moving too freely to be attached to a trap. As he reached over his rail, he gave the guys in Braxton's boat a wave. He snatched up the buoy, and the men froze, watching him. Tucker made a show of studying the straight-cut end of the line. *Wonder what's wrong with this picture, eh, fellas?*

Tom Braxton grabbed the wheel of his boat and pushed down on the throttle lever.

Tucker hollered at Braxton's broad backside, "'Ey-oh, Tom!"

The two deck hands turned their backs to the *Periwinkle*. Tucker tilted the throttle down all the way, and his boat leapt forward for a moment. Then he let up and steered alongside the *Water Angel*, less than an arm's length away.

Tom had no choice but to take notice of him. He left his boat in neutral and stuck his head out of the wheelhouse. "The hell you want, Flynn?" He was probably four hundred pounds, and his double chin shook as he barked at Tucker. His hair resembled steel wool, which he'd trapped within the red netting of a trucker hat. Deep-set blue eyes were cast in the shadow of overgrown silver eyebrow brambles.

Tucker cut his engine and stepped out of the wheelhouse to his rail, which was a long piece of plywood designed for the lobster traps. "Wanted to see if you knew anything about my two buoys over here—both of them cut. Seems like it must've happened just minutes ago." Tucker's words were slow and deliberate.

"Wouldn't know anything about that, Flynn," Tom said. "There was a boat in here when we came—sport boat, whizzing all over the fucking place. Kid driving. Maybe you should take it up with him. Little fucker drove toward the beach, if you're interested." Tom hooked his thumb back toward the Newborough State Beach, just beyond the harbor.

The two deckhands went right back to staring at Tucker. They held the same dry expression: glazed, dark eyes that didn't offer anything.

"Bullshit, Tom. You know as well as I do that these were cut intentionally. What the hell are you messing with my buoys for?"

The *Water Angel* was drifting away from Tucker's boat, so he grabbed a line and wrapped it around a cleat on the *Water Angel*. The two boats rocked against each other, peeling paint away as their sides rubbed, which was enough to get Tom to move his bulk out of the wheelhouse and stand in Tucker's face.

"Why don't you go find that sport boat, Flynn? 'Cause if

3

you're going to stick around here and piss me off, there's going to be more than lines cut." Tom's hands were on his wide hips.

The men on his boat stepped closer.

Tucker reached under the rail and scooped up the gaff. The aluminum pole was light, but the end held a fierce hook that was plenty sharp. Tucker had used the gaff to pull up sharks and tuna, but this was the first time he'd contemplated using it on a man. If the men aboard the *Water Angel* were at all intimidated by the gaff Tucker gripped like a staff, they hardly showed it.

A surge of adrenaline hit his toes then fired back up and slammed into his stomach. "Just because I don't want in on your greasy deals doesn't mean I'm going to be pushed around by you"—he jabbed a finger like a spear at Tom then turned it toward the deckhands—"or any of your friends, Braxton." Tucker's voice grew louder as he spoke.

Tom leaned closer to Tucker. His weight shifted his boat even harder against the *Periwinkle's* side, producing chirping sounds as fiberglass and wood rubbed together. "You're not thinking straight, Flynn. I'm one of the guys out here that actually likes you." Tom's fat face stretched wider when he smiled. Tom eyed the gaff then drew a gun from his pocket: a snub-nosed revolver whose black barrel stared at Tucker's chest. "But just because I like you doesn't mean I won't put you in your place."

Tom's finger latched on the trigger. Tucker's heart hammered against his rib cage, but he stood his ground.

"Put that gaff away. You look like a fucking farmer with a pitch fork."

The men behind Tom snickered, crossed their arms, and squared up. They muttered French to each other, a language Tucker had never had cause to learn. Tucker held eye contact with Tom, waiting for the standoff to be over.

Tom smiled then slipped the gun back in his pocket. "Doesn't have to be this way. I knew your father—figured he'd have knocked some sense into that thick head of yours. How much you still owe on that shack of his? More than it's worth I bet. No man worth his salt lets his wife pay the bills. Set an example for your boy."

4

Tucker gripped the gaff tighter. His legs were trembling.

"Get your head on straight—for your family's sake. You know where to find us." Tom turned around and headed back to his wheelhouse.

The deckhand with the knife nonchalantly leaned over the rail. "*Au revoir, petit homme.*" He cut the rope holding the two boats together without taking his eyes from Tucker's.

The *Water Angel* pulled away, and Tom called to Tucker, "I wouldn't waste my time checking your buoys off Seal Rock if I was you."

Tucker threw the gaff down and pounded his fist against the rail. He collected the cut buoy and snapped it in half over his knee. "Motherfucker! Piece of shit. Fat, fucking fuck, shit, fuck. Fuck. Fuck!" He slammed the butt of his fist on the rail with each word.

His boat remained in the cove, bobbing without a purpose. The storm clouds were now right above his head, and the wind was blowing over the dark waters, stirring a light chop. Instead of going back in, he went to check his last five buoys near Seal Rock, despite Tom. He wasn't surprised to find them missing.

Rain spit on his neck at first, then the clouds delivered an unrelenting downpour that made the sea bubble and foam. Tucker had it in his mind to go find Braxton's boat, pour a bucket of gasoline across the deck, and burn the vessel to ashes. He held on tight to that plan the whole way back to his slip. As he tied up to the dock, he saw his wife, Melanie, waiting for him under a black umbrella at her usual spot on the rail, just beyond the row of boats.

Seeing her standing there in the rain reminded him that he had more to lose than just himself. When he hugged her small frame tightly, he smelled, wafting from her curly hair, lavender shampoo, cigarette smoke, and citrus perfume. Her fingers dug into his shoulder blades and brought him back. Tucker abandoned the crazy idea and said nothing of what had happened out on the water.

# CHAPTER 1

ALTHOUGH JAMES HAD FOUGHT THE good fight, the hands of the clock still beat him. He shoveled a small stack of folders into his tattered leather suitcase. A wax-covered pamphlet slid out of one and onto his office desk. He flipped the paper around to see a child, but in place of its face was an apple. The apple had brown bruises and a pair of deep cuts across its red skin. The line above the image said, "Cuts and bruises are only okay on fruit." Below, in smaller print, a final line stated, "A message from New Hampshire's Association of Domestic Violence Youth Advocates." James shook his head. *Too bad we have to resort to shock imagery to get our point across.*

The phone rang. He considered transferring the call to the Concord office, but he thought better of it and slid the headphones back on his head. "New Hampshire Child Protective Services, this is James."

"Yeah, I, uh, I'm calling about a kid. Not mine, a friend's." The woman's raspy voice was painful to hear. He pictured a tired woman wrapped in a smoky haze.

James turned his computer screen back on and clicked to the Reports page. The pre-filled date on the form reminded him it was June 13, 2014. The dreaded Friday the Thirteenth. "What's your name, ma'am?"

"I want to remain anonymous. Only way I'll talk is if I'm anonymous."

"Okay, consider yourself anonymous. So I need the names of the family, the child, and an address. Why don't we start with that?"

"Jill Simmons. The father's not around. There's a boyfriend, Eddie Field, but he's locked up in county. Jill's daughter, the one who's being abused, Emily, she's four. They live in public housing — 18C Shad Drive in Newborough."

"Any other relatives around?"

"None that I know of."

He typed away and filled in the blank fields. "Tell me about Jill."

"Well, she's a druggie, I can tell you that: heroin, meth, pills. Whatever she can shoot up, sniff, or swallow."

"So she exposes Emily to drugs." James clicked a tab on the screen. "Okay, I need to figure out what kind of abuse Jill is doing. I'll go through a list, and you just tell me what fits."

"Okay."

He went through the list and got a pretty clear picture of Jill Simmons. She was an unemployed single mother living in government housing. She beat her daughter Emily, fed her alcohol to keep her quiet, left her alone and unattended for long periods of time, and Emily's health and hygiene were appalling. He'd filled in most of the boxes. The more boxes he checked off, the shittier the person was. So far, Jill had proved herself to be a monster.

"What happens next? Are you guys going to come and get Emily?"

"I'll file the report, and it'll be passed on to an assessment worker."

"That's it? You guys aren't going to come get her?"

"There will probably be an investigation, but I can't tell you much more than that, confidentiality and all."

"Oh."

"I can tell you this — I used to be one of the people who investigated cases like this. If things were as you described, I wouldn't rest until I got Emily out of that home and as far away from Jill as possible."

When he was done, he hung up and sent the report to a caseworker. Like most of his calls, he'd probably never know how the story ended, but experience cursed him with the assumption that Jill Simmons and her daughter, Emily, both had a long road to travel.

He didn't miss his years as a caseworker in the field. Those were long days where he cultivated anger and harvested sadness, watching as families would implode leaving innocence to rot like a dead cat on the side of the road. Answering phones and filing reports in a sterile office was fine by him.

James retrieved his small blue duffel bag from a shelf and hastily exchanged his button-down navy shirt and black tie for a plain white T-shirt. He dropped his black slacks to the floor and kicked off his tired-looking dress shoes. As he hauled up a pair of blue mesh shorts, his butt bumped against the single picture on his desk. The heavy silver frame whacked across the wood floor.

He hesitated then checked the damage. "Damn it."

A spiderweb of broken glass split across the wedding picture. His thumb rubbed the cracked glass, and he grinned, reliving the moment when Maya plowed cake into his mouth and rubbed in the frosting, using his face as a finger-paint canvas. White frosting stuck to his spike of black hair, the tip of his nose, and his clean-shaven goofily grinning face. He'd been quick to kiss her and smear cake across her brown skin, from her high cheekbones to her generous mouth.

James set the picture back in place, grabbed his cell phone off the desk, and hit speed dial. "Hey, I was thinking take-out tonight."

Voices muttered and yelled while phones rang in the background behind her.

"Funny. I was just about to call you. Get out of my head, Jamesey."

He could sense her smiling, and he envisioned her leaning back in her chair while the other police officers gathered witness testimonies at their desks or hammered the phones, following up on leads. He'd seen her department before and didn't envy her the stiff work atmosphere. He wanted to say something sexy, loosen her up, make her laugh.

He lifted his black sneakers and sniffed. "Oh, man." The smell of old sweat and dead skin made him wince, and like a squid out of water, the intimacy shriveled up and died.

"What?"

James dropped the Nikes and wiggled his feet into them. "Nothing. Hey, do we have any spare picture frames at home?"

"Let me guess, you broke the wedding picture again?" The higher pitch of her voice echoed her smug amusement.

"*Now* who's in whose head?" James chuckled.

Several loud voices echoed on her end.

"Hold on." After a five-second pause she said, "I think I have an extra frame in the closet. We thinking Chinese?"

He laced his sneakers and cradled the phone between his shoulder and cheek. "How about Thai? I'll call when I'm done at the rec center."

"I'll pick it up. Love you, Jamesey."

"I love you too." He tossed the phone and his work clothes in the duffel.

As he stepped outside his three-story office building, flashes of sunlight poked through the raised rectangles of brick and granite that dominated the greater downtown Newborough square. Tourists in plaid shorts and bright-colored polo shirts clung to the cobblestone sidewalks. Oftentimes they were Canadians who crossed the border to shop at the outlets in Kittery, Maine, or to strut their tanned bodies up and down the New Hampshire and Maine beaches.

James approached the only vehicle in the lot—his 150cc cherry-red moped, which he had grown to affectionately call Sally Jay. He tied the briefcase down tight with bungees and slipped on his shades and black half helmet, which Maya had nicknamed his "brain bucket."

Sally Jay whirred to life with a stiff kick-start, and he left downtown behind. The soup can mufflers rattled, and he caught a subtle whiff of gasoline. He twisted the throttle back and listened to the small engine strain and whine. The moped carved down the narrow streets lined with wooden clapboard colonials painted navy, pure whitewashed whites, and dark reds; the homes were so close that they almost leaned out over the road. The shadow of a church steeple cooled his skin. Like the rest of New Hampshire's tiny seacoast, the passing centuries had hardly touched the shape of Newborough.

As James turned a blind corner and picked up speed on the downhill, a car backing out of a driveway pushed its backside into his lane. James clenched his teeth and pushed the moped on a hard left slant, crossing the yellow lines and coming within a fingernail of smashing into the back of the wide Cadillac. The grill of an oncoming truck stared at him, and the horn blared. He swung his body and the handlebars right and nearly clipped the pickup truck's mirror. Back in his lane, the rearview showed the brake lights of the pickup truck's trailer, towing a white fiberglass fishing boat. The driver in the Cadillac, an old woman with large round glasses, hadn't even slowed.

A quick shot of adrenaline swam laps in James's veins. Ragged breaths blew out of his mouth, and his lungs worked as if they were being squeezed. *Not again. No!* He veered down a narrow side street, his neck stiff as rigor mortis. Tiny stabbing sensations pricked his scalp, and sweat slid down his jaw.

The alleyway transformed into a blur of light, concrete, and black shutters. His hands squeezed the rubber grips on the handlebars. He parked Sally Jay and slid down onto the cement, his shorts scraping against sand from last winter's plow trucks. "She could have killed me. Didn't even look. How could she be so stupid? Damn it!"

He removed his helmet and clutched it. As he squeezed, he heard a series of cracks, so he let the helmet tumble to the ground. He crossed his arms and held his sides, lips pressed together while he shook his head. All he could hear was the beat of his heart in his ears. His moist palms covered his face.

"Maya, Maya, Maya," he murmured like a mantra. He

pictured her lips across his face, her soft voice whispering to him.

The imaginary weight lifted from his chest. His pulse still raced but was beginning to coast. His breathing regained a rhythm. "I'm okay."

He wiped his brow, cleared his throat, and blinked. With a long sigh, he pushed off the cement and brushed off his shorts. His eyes scanned the house windows and the alley. No one had been watching, except for a lone seagull balanced on a trash can lid. He swallowed the trailing image of the moronic woman and got back on his moped.

He navigated to the edge of downtown and parked beside the granite steps to what had been a shoe factory in the early 1900s. The industrial brick building had been left vacant for decades, watching as Newborough became less and less seedy (formerly boasting a red-light district for the rowdy sailor boys hot off the clippers). A wealthy philanthropist named Theodore Monroe had put up his own money for the building's renovation and created a public basketball court. The rec center had evolved over the years and expanded to offer after-school and summer programming for local teens.

Inside the gym, James walked toward the rapping sound of dribbling basketballs, which echoed off the tan walls and into the rafters. James scooped up a rebound then passed the ball back to the shooter, a skinny boy named Adeeb. James slipped a white headband over his forehead.

Sweat glistened in Adeeb's short dark hair. He pulled up the bottom of his shirt, revealing a stomach with an "outie" belly button and a caramel complexion. "Want to play twenty-one, Mr. Jay?"

James nodded. "Go gather up the rest of the guys."

While Adeeb set out on his mission, James climbed the bleachers to the top row, where Derek Fanning was lying on his back and nodding to a beat. He paused his music, smiled at James, and sat up cross-legged.

"Derek, what's good?"

Derek brushed his long brown mop back over each of his

ears. "Everything's good, Mr. Jay. Listening to a band I think you'd like." He offered his headphones.

James sat next to him and slid the bulky headphones over his ears. A punk singer yelled over a fast drum beat. Snares crashed and the guitars whined while the singer bellowed half-discernable lyrics.

"I like it," James pinched out the lie and handed the headphones back.

"Band's called Cockerdoodle and the Dos. They're local."

James nodded and rubbed the sandpaper stubble on his chin. "I haven't seen you around. How's your summer been?"

Derek's fingers fondled a fat rubber band on his thin wrist. He twisted and snapped the band against his skin "Eh, it's all right, I guess. Been hanging out with some new people. Not sure how much I like them yet."

"Mr. Jay, are you playing or what?" Adeeb yelled.

A group of junior high boys trotted out of the rec room and onto the court. Fenton, a wiry kid sporting a fresh buzz cut, chased CJ, a chubby kid who swung his forearms like Popeye as he ran. The triplets, three boys walked out together. Behind the triplets, Trent, who wore an oversized black T-shirt that almost covered his knees, walked with a swagger while his best friend, Teddy—who stood at least a foot taller than Trent—laughed at something then tucked away his braces-smile. A stray girl, Tina—who wore ripped jeans and a low-cut black shirt littered with sparkles—gripped Adeeb's hand. Tina and Adeeb must be back together. *Guess that talk we had last week was a waste of breath, eh, Adeeb?*

Four girls with painted faces and ear-splitting laughs left the rec room, but instead of joining the game, they clustered at the edge of the court and punched at their cell phone screens with their thumbs. *Put the damn phones away and talk to each other.*

James clapped the bleacher. "Feel like playing, Derek?"

"Nah." He waved James off as he lay back down on the bleacher and resumed listening to his music.

There was a new young man on the court. James was struck

by an immediate sense of kinship for the short boy with a sunburned nose and cheeks. He had a nervous smile, and his blue eyes darted to each of his friends, as if trying to emulate their attitudes. James empathized with all the kids at the center, but something seemed familiar about this one in particular. James was about to introduce himself when a basketball bounced off his bad rib, leaving behind a stabbing sensation. He grinded his teeth, closed his eyes, and bent over.

"Sorry, I thought you were ready." Adeeb came over and collected the ball. "You okay?"

James grunted and waved in Adeeb's direction. *Son of a bitch, that hurt. Keep it cool, keep it together. I'm okay. Smile through the pain.* He stood back up. "Fine, let's play."

They played for an hour, then the director of the rec center dropped in and shook James's hand.

"Sorry about the sweat, Brian. This crew you've got here really put me to work."

Brian's brown eyes came alive through his thick lenses. "I give you credit. I haven't been able to play with these guys in years." He clapped his bulbous stomach like an old friend. "How's the social work business, James?"

"Booming, unfortunately. I'm busier than ever."

Brian shook his head. "You hear they had to cut twelve teachers at the high school? Good teachers too, the fresh ones who actually give a damn."

"How about here? Is the center still getting funding?"

"We're okay. This year, at least. You know I'll fight like Custer to keep us afloat next year."

*Don't remember it ending that well for Custer.* "The kids really love this place," James said. "Some like it better than home, I expect. Too bad the center wasn't around when I was growing up."

Brian's plump cheeks pushed his eyes closed as he chuckled. "Who you kidding? You may be in your thirties, but you're still growing up, Mr. Red Moped."

James grinned and elbowed Brian. "You sound like my wife."

"Now, *there's* a grown-up."

The boys came over and conned him into playing another game of 21. When it was over, the girls shuffled outside and the boys followed. The night air greeted James by sliding underneath his shirt and brushing against his sweaty skin like tongues licking his back. A solitary street lamp turned the pavement orange. James hung around the cluster of kids and watched as the younger ones caught rides from their parents. Several teens walked home. Derek mounted his bike and slapped James's hand as he pedaled by.

In the middle of the granite steps sat the new boy, the last one left.

"Anyone sitting here?" James asked.

"Nope."

James couldn't pin why the kid looked so familiar. James slipped a dark-blue University of New Hampshire sweat shirt over his head. "I didn't get a chance to properly introduce myself during the game. I'm James. Where did you learn that sweet hook shot?"

"Kevin. My brother taught me. He's dead." Kevin rubbed at a black scuff mark on his white sneaker.

"I'm sorry to hear that, Kevin." James rested his elbows on his knees and placed his chin on his fists. "Hurts to lose someone, doesn't it?"

He nodded and stared straight ahead.

"Who's picking you up?"

Kevin sighed. "My dad was supposed to pick me up, but he's late." He crossed his arms over his knees, holding his small biceps. His short sleeves shifted and revealed two fresh bruises on his right shoulder.

"Wow, look at those puppies." James pointed and said, "How'd you get those?"

He pulled his sleeve back down. "A bully from my neighborhood."

Several more bruises dotted his scabbed legs.

"What about the ones on your legs?" James asked.

14

Kevin spoke to his hands. "The same bully gave me those too."

If he was a liar, he was a good one. "You tell anyone about it?"

"My parents are too busy working."

"What do your parents do?" James asked.

Kevin shifted his expression. His chin lifted, and he offered a crooked bucktoothed smile. "You ask a lot of questions. My dad's a lobsterman."

"That's cool." James nodded and raised his eyebrows. "What's your mom do?"

"She's a waitress." Kevin's tone wasn't as enthusiastic. He looked James in the eyes for the first time. "What do you do?"

"I'm a social worker. I help families fix their problems."

Kevin nodded and seemed to consider the response. After a few moments, he asked, "Do you help people keep their houses and stuff like that?"

*This kid has a few layers.* James was about to answer, but the boy's attention turned to the old green Ford truck pulling up.

"There's my dad," Kevin said as he gathered his backpack. "I got to go."

James slowly followed Kevin, who ran to get into the truck. Kevin's dad unrolled his window as James came over. The familiar odor of fish emanated from within the cab. *That takes me back.* "Hi, I was just talking to Kevin here. He's got a heck of a hook shot."

The man turned to the passenger seat and rubbed his son's mop of hair. "Gets it from his old man. I used to shoot around when I was younger." He lifted the brim of his blue hat, which sported a smiling fish skeleton on the front.

James offered his hand. "James Morrow. I volunteer here at the center."

"Tucker Flynn." Tucker had a powerful handshake, and his calloused palm was among the roughest James had ever held. James's hands were petal-soft in comparison.

"Kevin tells me you're a lobsterman. How long you been doing that?"

Tucker looked at his son and back at James. "All my life. I inherited my dad's boat and traps and have been trying to scrape away a living ever since." Tucker checked the clock on the dash. "What kind of work you in?"

"I work for the city as a social worker specializing in domestic violence and child protection. Give me a second." James stepped over to his moped and relieved his briefcase of a business card. He passed the card to Tucker. "If you know anyone who needs some help, tell 'em to call me."

"Ah, you're one of them baby snatchers, huh?" Tucker said with a sadistic smile.

James had heard it all. He used to be offended when people bad-mouthed his job, then he learned to just be numb to the hate. *They despise us until they need us.* "Used to be. Spent eight years knocking on doors. Now I just field phone calls and process paperwork—less stressful, less pay, but I'm happy."

"I hear that. Listen, I got to get going before my wife starts to wonder where we are. Have a good one, James."

"Sure thing—hey, this is just a thought." James put his hand on the cool metal below the truck window. "Do you ever take people out on your boat? I've always wanted to go out on one— kind of a bucket-list thing, you know?"

"Not usually." Tucker rubbed the brim of his hat. "But, I mean, if you wanted to tag along this upcoming Sunday, it wouldn't bother me."

"Really? That's awesome. Count me in!" James said.

They quickly worked out the details, and James listened as the loose exhaust pipe rattled when Tucker and Kevin drove away.

James thought again about Kevin's bruises. "It's worth looking into."

# CHAPTER 2

THE CRASH OF THE BATTERING ram smashing through the front door reminded Maya that it was time to be alert. She rubbed her eyes and focused on the SWAT team charging through the doorway.

She leaned over the top of her cruiser, her Glock 19 drawn and the barrel aimed at one of the front windows of the chipped, scarred, and flaking colonial. A short, low-pitched bark, accompanied by a deep growl, emanated from inside the house. She shifted her chest, trying to readjust the vest beneath her shirt, and blinked rapidly. Her eyes were burning. The last few weeks were catching up to her. But Wade's informant had come through, so when the chief gave the okay to raid the Vasquez brothers' stash house, the entire department scrambled to get going. Friday the thirteenth was a horrible day for a raid.

"Police! Police! Warrant!" the men in body armor yelled as they charged into the house single file.

Maya watched the last man rush through the doorway, then she and her fellow officers charged past the chain-link fence and toward the porch steps. The distinctive boom of a shotgun blast set off a chorus of popping gun fire and confused shouts. Maya wasn't a firm believer in God, but she did believe in her gun and her strength; she was counting on them to keep her safe. She welcomed the adrenaline that kept her eyes open wide and awakened every cell of her body.

One of the two patrolmen running behind her yelled, "Go, go, go!"

She put together the scene in an instant. A dead German

shepherd lay in the middle of the living room shag carpet, the dog's fur matted with dark blood and parts of its pink insides visible. A piece of black fabric was in the dog's clenched jaws. The air smelled like a shooting range, and blood and bullet holes dotted the walls and furniture. The sofa was tacky — worn, upholstered in rust-red chrysanthemums and mustard-colored sunflower petals with charred seeds that belonged in the sixties — and it might have been the nicest thing in the room. A tipped-over, antique, cracked-leather brown chair lay pocked with bullet holes.

One SWAT officer, writhing on the floor and moaning, turned his face to reveal a man in his early thirties, wearing safety glasses. His cheeks were flushed, and he cradled what remained of his left arm. His forearm had been replaced with raw hamburger. He clutched the shattered mess and trembled. A fellow SWAT officer and two patrolmen helped him to his feet.

The man who'd shot the injured officer wasn't as lucky. His demolished face and torso resembled a beat-to-shit piñata.

The SWAT team had stopped behind a wall toward the back of the house. The rattle of an automatic weapon and a hail of bullets forced back the men.

"He's bunkered down in the room at the end of the hallway!" Captain Dennis Pharrel yelled, cupping a hand over his left ear.

Maya stood behind them. Captain Pharrel pulled out a flash bang grenade, released the pin, and pitched it like a baseball down the hall. A moment later, an explosive boom shook the walls. The gunfire ceased and was replaced by a man screaming in Spanish. Maya spied the unarmed shooter as he stumbled out of the room on his knees, hands covering his face on the floor. The SWAT team funneled down the corridor. Maya assumed their place watching as the men fell on the stunned attacker and held him down. Captain Pharrel forced the man's hands behind his back. They handcuffed him, and he bucked like a fish out of water.

"Stop resisting, you fucker! Stop resisting, damn it!" another SWAT officer screamed.

As Maya watched the men deal with the shooter on the floor, a false section of the drywall opened up in the corridor between her and the SWAT team. Ten feet in front of her, a man with a submachine gun stepped out and turned toward the SWAT officers. Maya aimed and rattled off four shots. The man fell away as all four bullets pierced him. Three hit his torso, and the recoil of her gun made one of the bullets fly high and travel through the back of his head. He dropped like a bag of concrete mix. The SWAT team raised their guns at Maya, who was still facing the man she'd killed.

The SWAT officer closest to the body, a towering man with cleft chin and a hooked red scar under his left eye, asked, "Where did that dirty fucker come from?"

Maya nudged her gun at the section of wall he'd come through.

"Jeez, damn spics crawling all over this fucking place," he muttered, shaking his head.

She doubted he would be showered with awards from the Latino community any time soon. The remaining SWAT and patrolmen that had searched through the house came back and announced that the rest of the rooms had been cleared.

Maya holstered her weapon. She walked up to the body of the man she'd killed and recognized him from his mug shot—Juan Vasquez. Blood leaked out of him, staining the dirt-caked carpet. She'd done the right thing; she'd followed her training and probably saved their lives, but a dead man lay at her feet, his eyes still open. *I'm good.* She said the words over and over in her head. Blood was seeping through the holes she'd put in him. She forced herself to shift her gaze. There were three SWAT officers on top of the stunned shooter, Ricky Vasquez. They worked hard to restrain him. Even in cuffs, he proved hard to handle. Ricky spit on the scarred officer's shoe. Seeing the bloody phlegm on his polished boot, the officer tucked in his lower lip and kicked Ricky in the ribs. Ricky grunted and closed his eyes.

Adding insult, the officer rubbed the spit off on Ricky's face, saying, "You like that? Huh?"

"That's enough!" Maya pointed at the scarred officer. "What's your name?"

He switched his grip on his M-16 rifle. "Dale Patterson, with two Ts."

*What a prick.* "Patterson, I'll be sure to remember that. Now get out of here. And will one of you fine officers read Ricky his rights and put him in a squad car?"

Patterson gave her a look as if he'd just bitten into a rotten pear, then he turned to Captain Pharrel with a wry smile. "There's a reason she's the only woman on scene, Cap."

Captain Pharrel nodded to Patterson. "Do as she says."

Patterson wiped his lips with gloved fingers and shook his head. As he walked by her, he nudged his arm against her right shoulder.

*Oh no, not today.* She pivoted and snapped her fingers at Patterson. "Don't make me sorry that I saved your life!"

He walked down the hall and muttered something, but she couldn't make out the words.

The remaining officer on top of Ricky must have been watching her and Patterson go at it, because he was frowning in her direction.

Maya pulled Ricky up off the ground. "Since none of you can seem to handle this, I'll take him in."

Ricky saw his brother lying dead. "You're fucking dead, bitch."

"Where are the drugs coming from, Ricky?" Maya asked.

"Up your black ass, you fucking *puta*!"

"You kiss your mother with that mouth?" Sam said. As the only other black detective in Maya's department, he always had her back.

He grabbed Ricky's other elbow, and together they led him out of the house. A small crowd of neighbors and spectators had gathered, kept at bay by a ring of squad cars and police. A reporter with a "press" vest snapped pictures from across the street. A news crew was trying to set up a camera just beyond the yellow tape.

*How did they get here so fast?*

"You just made a lot of enemies," Ricky said.

Maya ignored him. They crossed the porch, went down the steps, and led him across the walkway. Sam read Ricky his rights.

"Do you understand?" Maya echoed.

Ricky lunged backward, twisting his body, and tried to bite Maya's neck.

"Hey, Sam!" She dodged his teeth while Sam pulled him away.

Ricky turned on Sam, head-butting him. Sam stumbled, clutching his forehead. Without hesitation, Maya tripped Ricky and slammed him to the ground. With his hands cuffed behind him, Ricky had no way to buffer his fall. Maya dropped her knee into his back. Two patrolmen rushed to her aid. *About time someone gets off their asses and helps.*

Charlie, the newest Newborough patrolman, and his training officer, a hawk-faced old veteran named Sarah, lifted Ricky off the sunburnt lawn, his face and mouth oozing fresh blood. Charlie and Sarah hauled him into the nearest squad car. From behind the glass, Ricky laughed as he wiped his bloody face all over the inside of the window.

Captain Pharrel came over and put a hand on Maya's bicep. "Are you all right?"

"Yes." She shrugged off the captain's hand. "When he calms down, have the medics patch him up."

Captain Pharrel widened the gap between his black boots. "Listen, I'm sorry for how Patterson acted in there. He was right behind Jacobs when they popped out with the shotgun. A guy sees that, and it messes with his head." His finger rotated beside his head momentarily. "He was still in attack mode. Don't worry, he'll be dealt with. You have my word on that."

Maya squared up and crossed her arms. "I'll be filing a complaint of my own. That was sloppy." Maya brushed a stray hair out of her eyes.

Captain Pharrel held his deadpan expression. "We found a

dropdown attic where they'd stashed the drugs. Found several packages of marijuana, pills, and cash. There were more guns under the mattresses."

Maya scratched her scalp and sighed. *No heroin?* "Think they knew we were coming?"

"Seems that way. Ricky was hunkered down tight, and the perp you shot had enough time to hide in the wall. Very elaborate, I'll give them that."

"How's your man... Jacobs, was it?" Maya asked. "How's his arm?"

"They hauled him off in the ambo. I don't know his status yet. Was a mess from what I saw."

Maya turned to see Chief Gary McCourt step out of the passenger side of a squad car. He assumed command of the scene the second his shoe touched asphalt. His driver, Detective Wade Copley, followed as the chief walked from one uniformed officer to another.

"Gentry, I want the bodies covered. Ellis, scatter those people and tell the press to call me for an official report," the chief said. "Ted, get some lights set up. It'll be dark soon." Each order was accompanied by a pointed index finger and a willing officer hustling off to carry out the task. Chief McCourt rubbed his neat mustache and came over to Maya. "Wade and Sam will go through the house and make a report. I want everyone else off this crime scene." McCourt took her aside and, in a hushed voice, said, "Heard you discharged your weapon. You all right?"

"I'm fine."

"It's okay to admit if you're not. Even seasoned guys get pretty shaken up over that sort of thing."

"Chief..."

"A paperwork nightmare."

She spoke louder, "Sir, I'm going to be filing a complaint against one of the SWAT officers. He kicked and antagonized the man I arrested."

The chief sighed and wiped a hand through his silver thinning

22

hair. "Listen, Maya, I need you to let that go. Even though a lot of them are on our payroll, these SWAT guys deal with their own. A complaint isn't going to help with their funding, and face it, we might need these guys again in the future. Besides, there are far worse things than a kick to a man resisting arrest."

"I don't think—"

He put a hand on her shoulder. "Drop it." His tone shifted from soft to rough. "I will make sure this gets dealt with correctly. Right, Captain?"

Captain Pharrel, who'd been quietly waiting, gave a slow, emphatic nod.

The chief came closer to her face and lowered his tone again. "So you know, since you killed the suspect, that you'll have to take the next few weeks off duty while they clear you, right?"

"Weeks? I thought it was just three days?" Even if they hadn't cleared her, the rules said she could still work after three days.

"Technically, yes, you can work while they're investigating, but it might be easier to wait till internal affairs clears you."

"You mean Wade?" With a department as small as Newborough's, Wade was their only internal affairs officer.

"Yeah, Wade's a good old boy. He'll get you through the interviews and try to rush you through quick. But you still need the lawyer, psychiatrist, and all the rest. Talk to Sergeant Duncan. The scene's safe, so you're officially off duty until you're cleared." The chief clapped once then rubbed his palms. "Now, let's go see what they were protecting in this house."

Maya couldn't help feeling wronged, but McCourt had always proved a fair man. As chief of police, he would make sure that Patterson's insubordination was dealt with. She watched him move in short strides up the walkway. The adrenaline had left her. Her training had helped her pull the trigger, but she was hardly prepared for the end result. She was now a killer. *No. Not today.* She couldn't appear weak, not now, with all the men watching her.

She bit a chunk of her cheek, wiped her eyes, and went to find Sergeant Duncan.

# CHAPTER 3

J AMES OPENED THE DOOR TO his two-story condo only to find darkness awaiting him. He kicked off his dress shoes at the entrance and climbed the carpeted stairs. Along the wall were pictures. One frame, hanging off-center, held a photo of the Newborough Police Department. As a black woman, his wife stuck out among the rows of uniformed white guys. The only other black person in the department was Sam. James straightened the crooked picture and headed into the bedroom. He set his briefcase on top of Maya's gun safe, which was gray and the size of a dorm mini-fridge. James stared at the digital code box. What a pain in the ass that had been to haul up there when they moved in three years earlier.

He remembered the first time he and Maya had gone shooting at the range. She'd been impressed by his ability to handle her handguns. Time after time, his bullets tore through the paper target, leaving behind tight groupings — tighter than hers. For him, it was a useless skill, one he'd learned after years of shooting his father's guns in the sand pits on the outskirts of Newborough.

In the shower, he removed a disc of long black hair that was clogging the drain then let the hot water wash his skin. Afterward, wearing nothing but shorts, James sank deep into his corner of the downstairs couch. He flicked through a couple of movies and ended up settling on the local news. He was getting drowsy when the sound of jingling keys worked the front door lock. James sprang up and rushed to open the door.

Maya's silhouette, with a bag of Thai food, appeared in

front of him. As she came inside, she said, "Dark in here." Her fingers brushed a panel of switches.

James squinted against the light. Maya set down the food, slid her keys and phone across the counter, and stripped off her suit jacket and blouse as she climbed the stairs. Minutes later, she came down in cotton shorts and a T-shirt without a bra. On the couch, she lay against his chest and sighed.

He clasped her hand and rubbed his thumb in small circles over her knuckles. "How was your Friday the thirteenth?"

She sighed again. "I don't want to think about it. I just want to lay here."

"Another tough one, huh?"

"Yup, now shush." Maya adjusted her head on his shoulder.

He breathed in the scent of grapefruit and vanilla from her hair. He thought he caught a whiff of gunpowder.

After finishing his pad thai, James turned his attention to the news as the snub-nosed, blond anchorwoman segued into the next story. "Earlier this evening, a twenty-six-year-old man in Backbury, Massachusetts, attacked his mother and two sisters with a machete, killing the mother and one of the girls. The surviving eight-year-old girl is currently in critical condition in Massachusetts General."

They played interviews with the neighbors.

An overweight woman with her arms crossed under her ample chest spoke while shaking her head. "I can't believe it. I see him every day. He's always been such a nice guy."

"They always say 'he's a nice guy,'" Maya said. "But those are the ones you have to look out for." She cleared the dishes and the plastic takeout boxes from the coffee table.

James tasted bitterness as the report reconstructed the scene. "Hey, I'm a nice guy. You don't see me running around on a killing spree."

The anchorwoman had thrown to a weak-jawed young man named Chris Agnew, broadcasting beside the busy Mass Pike. "Massachusetts and New Hampshire state troopers have been on the lookout for traffickers of an old drug that's finding a new home. The neighboring states are working hand-in-hand with detectives and narcotics task force teams on both sides of the state line in an effort to halt the spread of what many consider the worst opiate on the market: heroin."

Chris Agnew commenced an off-screen interview. "I thought heroin had declined after the '70s?"

The curly-haired man being interviewed wore silver-framed glasses and a powder-blue shirt. "Yes, you're right. It certainly dropped off the map for a while. However, heroin is making a strong resurgence, and not just in cities but in rural areas too."

Chris Agnew asked, "Why is this happening now, in 2014?"

"One connection that we see is the higher costs of prescription pain pills. Many addicts start out taking painkillers, but that's an expensive habit. Heroin, however, is cheap and available. This isn't just a city problem anymore — it's moved to the suburbs and rural areas." The guest stared directly into the camera and pointed. "I'd bet that many of your viewers living in rural New Hampshire, Maine, and Vermont know someone struggling with a heroin addiction right now. It's time for us as a society to discuss this issue, not cover up the problem. One day, maybe we'll treat addiction as an illness, not a crime."

Chief McCourt's mustached face came into focus. He was flanked by police officers as he spoke into five different microphones.

The anchorwoman said, "At a public conference held yesterday in New Hampshire, Newborough Police Chief Gary McCourt spoke out about his plan to combat the trafficking and illegal sale of heroin."

"There's my boss," Maya said.

Although they weren't friends, James had met McCourt several times. The man was a slow talker who always seemed impeccably clean and composed. When he raised his eyebrows, four long trenches sprouted across his forehead. His thinning silver hair was cut military standard, high and tight, like many of the officers around him. James caught the tail end of what McCourt was saying.

"The best thing we can do is to spread the information so

that the public is aware of the dangers of using heroin and other harmful drugs. At this time, we're working very closely with several police departments and are confident in our plans to halt the trafficking into the Granite State of this highly addictive and lethal drug."

"Too late for that, I'm afraid," James said.

The feed flipped back to the anchor room.

Maya cast a deep frown his way. "I know you've seen your share of drug problems at work, but this is different. It's becoming an epidemic."

"Always is." James smiled.

Maya rolled her eyes and turned off the TV. She curled into his chest, and they kissed. She had coffee breath, but he didn't care.

James held her sleepy gaze. Goose bumps prickled about his skin. Maya's eyes opened wide like window shades; she released her hair from the tightly-coiled bun. The black hair fell over her face. The warmth of her hands smoothed his chilled skin and stirred his nerves. Wordlessly, they each stripped off their own clothes. Maya kissed him hard, her teeth holding him prisoner by his lower lip. A quick pinch to her hip got her to release. She pushed him onto his back. As he attempted to right himself, she pushed him down again. *It's going to be like that, huh?*

James met her focused eyes. She kept her hand on his chest while she straddled him. The warmth of their centers met. His fingertips skimmed over her nipples, then he squeezed her two soft mounds of breast. Her back arched while her chest rose and fell with each breath. As he moved to slip into her, she grabbed his dick, shook her head, and smiled.

"You're a damn tease, woman."

She nodded and rubbed against him faster. The friction made his heart beat faster. The heel of her hand pushed down against his chest.

An intense line of pain radiated from his lower chest. "Ouch! Stop, bad rib, my bad rib, babe."

She pulled her hands away. "I'm sorry. I forget sometimes."

The pain settled to a dull throbbing. "No problem, my love." James kissed her again and searched with his tongue. James slowly eased his body into hers. The couch was as good a place as any.

Maya shuddered then cooed. She rode him fast and hard. Her loose hair bounced and swung across her face. James watched as her eyes closed, and she scrunched up her features. James squeezed her hips, tracing old stretch marks as he thrust. It was Maya who released the first sigh. James's followed soon after. James, still tucked within her, relished the fading sensations.

He gave her a wink. "I have a good feeling about that one, babe."

Maya punched his shoulder. "Heard that before."

"Takes time—"

Maya pressed her index finger to his lips and shushed him. "Please don't try to tell a woman about how pregnancy works."

"All right, I won't. Just saying, that was baby-making sex right there." He laughed and slung his arm around her.

They both breathed in the damp, still air of their hotbox apartment. The open windows offered only humidity. Their slick bodies lingered on the polyester cushions.

"I'm glad I can be your stress ball." James flashed her a grin.

"I told you I had a tough day."

"Feel better?" He wiped sweat off his forehead and onto the nape of her neck.

"I feel great now." She sighed as she said the words. Maya smiled and patted his chest.

James licked his lips and shifted his chest to watch her. "It happened again today."

Her eyes opened, and she planted her chin on his sternum. "What? *Oh*! You all right?"

"Yeah, a car almost hit me. I had to pull over. Saw red again."

"You make me nervous on that stupid moped. I wish you'd use my car in the summer."

James lifted his eyebrows.

"Well, you already know how I feel. They make cops see psychiatrists. It's no big deal."

"I think I have a handle on it now." He kissed her warm lips.

"I love you more than anything on this planet, Jamesey, but you have to admit that you've got some anger issues to work out."

"If they get to be more than I can deal with, I'll see a doctor — promise."

She curled her pinkie finger, and he hooked his curled pinkie in hers.

"Speaking of issues and doctors... your rib still hurts after all these years, huh?" Maya traced his bottom right rib with her index finger.

James touched the tender bone. "One of the last reminders of Dad."

Maya combed her fingers through his hair. "I have the next three days off. Let's do something fun this weekend. What about Sunday?"

James opened his eyes. "Can't Sunday."

"Why? What are you doing Sunday?"

"I'm going fishing." James scratched her back and watched her eyes close. He heard her release a heavy sigh. "Wait, why do you have the next three days off?"

"I... shot a man... today."

James stopped rubbing Maya's back and turned her so she faced him. "What? You what? Why am I just hearing about this now? Is he...?"

"He's dead. It was during a drug raid. He had a gun."

"Jesus." James wrapped his arms around her and squeezed. He searched her body with his eyes. Why hadn't she told him sooner? She'd killed a man — that must affect her.

"See, this is why I didn't want to talk about it."

"Are you okay?"

"I'm fine. It's part of the job. It's why I carry a gun every day."

"Yeah, but this is the first time it's happened. I'll stay home with you."

Maya frowned. "No. Besides, I have meetings, and I won't be here much. I'll be busy, don't worry." She pressed three fingers into his shoulder. "Go to work, go fishing. Let's just try to keep this as normal as possible."

"I wish I could have been there with you." James kissed her cheek.

"I'm glad you weren't," Maya said.

"Please tell me right away when something like this happens. I can't believe I was going on about my petty bullshit." James shook his head.

Maya shushed him. "I like hearing about your day. That's normal to me."

"God, I love you so much, Maya." He hugged her and held her.

"I love you more," Maya whispered in his ear.

# CHAPTER 4

SUNDAY ARRIVED, AND JAMES FOUND himself parking Sally Jay on the loose gravel lot of Denny's Clam Shack, a local seafood restaurant and bar. Denny's was built on Crooked Creek, an outlet to the Skog River, which dumped into the Atlantic Ocean. He breathed in the smell of baking peat and drying seaweed mixed with brackish river water. Around the backside of the restaurant, a catwalk lay suspended over the exposed tidal mud. He leaned against the dry, splintered railing leading down to the docks. The resting boats, lined up like waterfowl, were an eclectic flock. Flashy sport boats floated alongside double-deckers rigged up for deep sea fishing. James's eye was drawn to a sleek cigarette boat with a glossy wooden hull and tight-knit green fabric seats.

The boat was the same style as the one his childhood friend Nick Fahrenheit's dad had owned. Nick's father used to take the two boys out on the water every summer. One day James had gotten into an argument with Nick over whose turn it was to get pulled behind the boat on the inner tube. James remembered throwing his friend to the deck of the boat and wind-milling his fists into Nick's frightened eyes. Mr. Fahrenheit, a tall, naturally athletic man, had hauled James off his terrified son by his life vest and immediately thrown James overboard. He yelled at James over the railing, telling him to "cool off," and calling him "a little psychopath." James remembered thinking Mr. Fahrenheit would leave him there in the middle of the Skog; instead, he'd lifted James back on the boat and brought him straight home.

Before James got out of Mr. Fahrenheit's car that day, for what would be the last time, the man had looked James straight in the eyes and said, "I know it's not *all* your fault, kid." James could still remember the way Mr. Fahrenheit had eyed James's dad's rust-stained white Chevy truck in the driveway. "I won't tell your dad. We all know he'd probably whup the shit out of you for this." Mr. Fahrenheit shook his head at his words. "But I can't have you hanging around Nick anymore."

James shrugged off the sour memory and surveyed beyond the cigarette boat to where Tucker waved at him. Dad had done one thing right—he'd shown James how anger and violence only led to pain and despair. James had vowed to live a gentle life, to advocate for kids, and had discovered over the years that rewards came with the peace. James pushed away from the railing and walked down the gang plank to meet Tucker.

James sized up the boat and read the hand-painted letters out loud. "The *Periwinkle*."

"Beauty, ain't she?" Tucker said.

"She's impressive. Permission to come aboard, Captain?"

"None of that 'captain' crap. Just get your ass in here before I take off without you."

Tucker got the boat's engine going, and James untied the dock lines from the cleats. Taking command in the wheelhouse, Tucker drove his boat with an experienced hand, gliding downriver, hugging each marker buoy like an old acquaintance.

Even though the *Periwinkle* wasn't built for speed, more of a workhorse really, it still cut the water with sharp pride, leaving behind only a subtle wake. Luxurious homes dotted each side of the creek. Some were half-hidden, others laid out for full view, almost saying, "Judge me, I dare you." Their well-manicured lawns led down to long, sun-cooked docks whose posts were driven deep into the loose river mud. Tree branches stuck out of the water on either side of the river, and rocks poked just above the water, supporting small mats of floating seaweed along both shores.

Through tinted lenses, James glanced at the bold sun directly above their heads. The light scattered across the water's surface like handfuls of pixie dust. Gulls called and beat their bent wings above them while some landed on the green-and-red marker buoys. James noticed some gulls dropping crabs and snails onto the docks to crack the shells and pulling away meat.

"This was my father's boat," Tucker said. "I fixed her up and got her seaworthy again after he died. My dad was a poor New Hampshire lobsterman and looks like I am too."

"My dad processed fish. I remember, as a kid, always wondering why refrigerators were built so big when ours held so little." No lies there. "Are things extra tough for you right now?"

Tucker sighed. "The bank is giving me sixty days to clear out of my childhood home. We're worse than broke. My parents left me the house, which was really just a boatload of debt. No pun intended. The one thing they ever managed to pay off was the *Periwinkle* here." He massaged the wheel as if petting the ear of a loyal dog.

"She's a beautiful lobster boat, the finest I've ever been on."

Tucker laughed. "How many lobster boats you been on?"

"This would be my first."

They shared a laugh. Tucker drove down the Skog River's main channel, showing James where the high tide covered hidden sand bars and rocks. James's thoughts swung back to why he was there in the first place. He pictured Tucker's son, Kevin. So far, there wasn't much of a case.

As they cleared the rock jetties that marked the mouth where the river and ocean met, cool air blew past James's face. Tucker stood tall, eyed the water, and kept an ear tuned to the sounds of the boat's engine. The *Periwinkle* seemed to respond to his careful touch, a mutual respect between man and machine.

"Hold on to your hat, Jimmy. Going to give her some gas."

James watched Tucker turn his dirty Red Sox cap backward, so James did the same with his flimsy "Life is Good" hat. Tucker eased the throttle lever down and made some wake. The water churned, the propeller stirring up foam like a blender.

The motor hummed with a higher pitch while the bow rose to ride the ocean chop.

Tucker pushed farther into open water, his squinting eyes searching. He yelled over the noise of the motor, "You see them?"

James peered over the ocean waves and noticed the distant islands of the Isles of Shoals to the northeast. *See what?*

Tucker slowed the boat down and pointed ahead. "You see those birds?"

James scanned the air until he glimpsed specks in the distance. They hovered together, then one bird dove headlong into the sea. Others followed. Their winged bodies speared into the ocean, then they rose up from the depths with silver fish flopping in their beaks.

"They're called terns. The birds, they're my eyes," Tucker said. He winked again, spinning the wheel sharply to the left. "Turn where the terns turn, and you'll find the fish," he sang.

Tucker slowed the boat and told James to grab one of the rods sticking out of the back. James picked one that had six shiny hooks dangling loosely. A weight hung at the bottom of the setup.

"That's a good rod. It's all rigged up with sabiki hooks."

James wasn't convinced. The thing seemed as if it was one wrong move away from a tangled mess. "What kind of fish are we going for?"

Tucker turned off the engine and let the boat drift. He tossed a few chunks of something into the water. "Mackerel, of course."

Tucker dropped his own sabiki rig into the water, and James followed. Tucker told him to jiggle the line every so often so the light would reflect off the lures. Within a minute, James felt something tugging at his line.

Tucker laughed and said, "Here we go," as if they were about to go down a water slide.

James reeled up his line and found that he actually had two somethings on his line. The blue-and-black striped fish dangling from the hooks flailed their tight bodies. James unhooked one while the other fish shook free, hitting the deck hard and flapping between James's legs.

Tucker grabbed the loose fish and tossed it into an orange bucket. A second later, Tucker's rod tip jumped.

"We're on the mackerel; hit a school of 'em. They make great lobster bait," Tucker said.

James nodded, realizing for the first time that they were catching their bait.

Two buckets full of mackerel and an hour later, as suddenly as the school of fish had come, they were gone, prompting the departure of the terns.

"We did pretty well. That ought to bait most of the traps we pull today." Tucker shoved the buckets toward the back of the boat.

James gripped the railing as Tucker put the boat in full gear and steered back toward the coast. The splashing sounds of the prow cutting through the waves combined with the wind that sounded as if someone was shaking a giant poster board.

The boat cruised along the coast. Tucker pointed at something ahead of them, and James followed the outstretched index finger. A cluster of rocks rising out of the ocean formed a tiny island no bigger than a parking space. A brown head lifted from the seaweed and gave the *Periwinkle* its attention.

"That's Seal Rock," Tucker said, squinting in the light. "They say seals carry the souls of those lost at sea." His tone was somber. "Kevin tell you about his brother, Jacob?"

"He did tell me he lost his older brother. I'm sorry for your loss."

Tucker tightened his lips and stared out the wheelhouse window. "Yeah, Jacob was a good boy. Kevin loved the hell out of his brother. He talks about him a lot. It's his way of keeping him alive or something. I don't know. When you lose a kid, you try to focus on what you have left. Good thing we have Kevin is all."

James nodded. How had Jacob died? Did Tucker think that

Kevin had already told him how? *At some point, I'm sure I'll find out.*

The *Periwinkle* hugged the coast for a while longer, and Tucker maneuvered her around lobster buoys. They slowed down and settled into a pack of buoys that bobbed as if they were seamen waiting to get rescued.

"See the blue-and-white buoy?"

James found the buoy Tucker was talking about.

"Lean over and grab it when we approach."

"Easy enough," James said.

When James leaned over, he saw the sandy bottom of the ocean floor. He snatched the buoy and pulled. A green-slime-covered rope came along with it. He held the buoy as if he had just won a huge, overstuffed bear. The slack of the rope began to go taut.

Tucker's instructions came quickly. "Put the rope through the pulley on the davit. No, not that way—this way. Yes, now pull. Yeah, it's slimy. Keep pulling. Try using your body and leaning back. Put your foot here. Yeah, that's the way. See the trap yet?"

James held the rope and peeked over the rail. The green cage hung just below the surface.

"Okay, now keep pulling," Tucker said. He caught the trap and, with one hand, slid it along a flat stretch of plywood built along the right side of the boat. "Now unhook that line and hook up this one. Nope, wrong way. Hurry up; we're starting to drift here."

James grinned. He felt as if he were a kid working his first job. He hauled up the rope, hand over hand. The slime made it hard to grip, and the salt water kept spraying in his eyes. Despite those annoyances, James heaved the rope and saw a second trap breach the surface. This time he anchored the rope by stepping on the line. He grabbed the hanging trap and handed it to Tucker. James reset the rope and hauled up the final trap that was linked to the other two.

For the first time, he actually peered inside the traps he'd pulled up. Black-speckled lobsters with undertones of green and orange thrashed against the walls. The dark lobsters crawled about, some retracting their tails violently, trying to escape their prison. James counted at least five lobsters in each.

"Look at all those suckers," James said.

"Yeah, let's see if we can get one or two keepers from this trawl."

"One or two?"

"I'll show you." Tucker whipped out a metal tool and grabbed a medium-sized lobster from the first trap. "You measure them by their carapace here. You see?" The lobster measured short by a hair. "That means this guy's no good." Tucker tossed the lobster back into the water. "All right, now take out all the lobsters that are obviously too small. If any seem close, make sure to measure them how I showed you." Tucker seized a handful of mackerel and began stuffing the trap bait bags.

Each trap captured a buffet of squirming, flipping, and crawling creatures. Big hulking crabs, snails, sea urchins, hermit crabs, starfish, and even tiny minnows had somehow been hauled aboard.

By the time James got rid of the small lobsters, he was left with four that appeared to be big enough. "These four look good, Tucker."

Tucker picked one up and spread its tail. "No good, this one's notched."

James examined the small V cut into its tail. "What? Like tagged?"

"Yeah, she's a breeder. They notch the females so that they can keep on breeding." Tucker let the struggling lobster fall into the water.

From the other three lobsters, one was a fraction too short and another one was notched as well. They were left with one keeper.

"That's about a pound and a half," Tucker told him.

"That's a lot of work for one lobster," James said.

"Fish and Game are pretty strict about what you can keep,

which makes it hard for the guys like me who set their traps close to shore instead of miles out. Government assholes! Don't get me started."

Tucker demonstrated how to band the claws so they wouldn't pinch. He put the keeper in a live well, baited the traps, then steered the boat back to their shallow spot. "When I tell you to, drop the first trap on the end there overboard. Try to drop it parallel to shore and flat."

When Tucker was satisfied with the spot, he said, "Go."

James threw the trap over and watched the bricks inside carry the trap down. The trap's rope coiled around James's right leg. The line began to tug. "Shit!"

James struggled to get the rope free and felt the line tighten, gripping his leg like a tourniquet. He tried to peel the rope off his calf, his fingers wedging between the rope and his leg, but the trap line's pull forced him to skip awkwardly backward. In his struggle, he grabbed the rope from over the side and tried to haul the trap back up, but with the boat still trolling, the line was far too heavy. He was dragged to the back of the boat. The rope was cutting his skin. James held himself in the boat while the roiling water a few feet below was diced up by the propeller blades. The rope wanted him to follow the trap, to go into the blender and pull him to the bottom.

"Help me!" he called.

Tucker cut the engine and rushed to the back of the boat. He grabbed the length of taut rope and pulled with all his weight. The rope gave some slack, and James slid his leg loose of the death grip and watched wide-eyed as the rope was carried away. His heart was trying to punch through his chest.

"Got to be mindful of where the rope is, James. It's one of those universal rules on any boat."

James wiped sweat out of his eyes, still astonished at how stupid he'd been. It had happened so quickly. How could he have been so stupid? His pulse fluttered, and his temples shook. *Maya, Maya, Maya.*

Tucker slid the last two traps off the rail and put a hand on James's shoulder. "Hey, you okay?"

James flung Tucker's hand off of him and leaned against the far rail. He gripped the fiberglass and stared at the dark-blue water. His molars creaked and ground together. When he closed his eyes, instead of black, he saw red. *Maya, please, Maya. I'm okay.* The seagulls' distant calls, the crashing waves, the idling motor.

He loosened his grip and cleared his throat. When he opened his eyes, he saw the dark blue of the open ocean and the clouds clumped like mashed potatoes on a plate of light blue. "Sorry about that, I—"

"I'd recognize that face anywhere."

James turned his attention to Tucker.

Tucker's eyes were on the sea ahead of him. "No big deal. Anger grabs me by the collar sometimes too." He scratched the wheel with his thumbnail. "But we have lobsters to catch. Another buoy's coming, and it's got your name written all over it." As if all previous moments had been blown out to sea, Tucker set James right back to work.

After a few more buoys, James was hauling traps, banding lobsters, and stuffing bait bags alongside Tucker. They caught plenty of keepers but threw back many more. One lobster James pulled out of a trap was loaded with thousands of tiny brown eggs under her tail.

"An egger. She's pregnant, have to throw her back." Tucker added, "Be gentle."

After James released the egger, he asked, "So what is this mechanical-looking wheel by the davit here?"

Tucker tossed him a smile and a wink. "Oh, that's the winch."

"You have a winch? How come you don't use it?"

"I use it, but I wanted to make sure you roughened up those soft, paper-peeling hands of yours." He burst into heavy laughter.

All James could do was smile at the bastard. His plan had succeeded. James flexed his hands and stared at his bright-red and raw palms.

They used the winch for the rest of the traps, which made the process much easier. When the light began to fade, they headed back toward the harbor, and Tucker told James to take the wheel. James's hands worked to find the right touch while Tucker cleaned the deck and stowed the lobsters and remaining mackerel in the hold. The *Periwinkle* tried to buck off course with each passing wave, and James had to fight to keep her in a steady line. James slowed down as they got to the mouth of the Skog and followed another fishing boat plowing up the channel.

James noticed a gray marine patrol boat spearing its prow in their direction. James instinctively slowed the boat to a crawl and pulled a little off to the right as if he were on the highway. "Tuck, I think marine patrol is pulling me over here."

Tucker, who had been bent over the side scrubbing bloody scales off the knife, stabbed the blade into the wooden plank and took over at the wheel. "What the hell do these jerk-offs want now?" He steered alongside the marine patrol's boat.

Two of the three men aboard wore black police uniforms with inflatable life vests horse-collared around their necks. The third man standing at the boat's railing, a Fish and Game conservation officer, wore a forest-green uniform shirt and army-green pants. They threw round, orange boat fenders over the sides of their patrol boat, and James tossed them the *Periwinkle's* lines. One marine patrol officer and the Fish and Game officer came aboard.

The marine patrol officer spoke first. "I'm Officer Ted Stevens." His voice was monotone. His black hat brim was pulled low, shading his brown eyes. He was probably in his early twenties, with a lean frame and a blocky face. "And this" — he pointed at the Fish and Game officer — "is Colonel Greg Bender." Officer Stevens nodded at Tucker. "You been lobstering or fishing today?"

Tucker left his boat in neutral. "I've been lobstering all day."

"Okay, well, we've received reports that your boat was seen driving recklessly."

Tucker shook his head and let his hand rise and fall to his hip. "Must be another boat. I've been driving fine."

"I'm going to need to see *both* of your boating licenses," Officer Stevens said.

Tucker showed him his. "This is my boat. I've been driving all day. This is a friend of mine. He's been helping me haul traps."

While still focused on Tucker, the officer pointed at James's chest. "I saw *him* driving, so if *he* doesn't show me a boating license, *he* is going to get a citation."

"The hell he is! He took the wheel for a second while I put a fucking bucket away." Tucker's fists squeezed at his sides while veins on his arms swelled under his skin.

Colonel Bender busied himself by inspecting various parts of Tucker's gear. He made several clicking noises and shook his head as he made a visual inspection of the *Periwinkle*. He examined the live well and snapped his fingers at Tucker. "This account for all your catch?" Colonel Bender scratched his strawberry-blond mustache.

Tucker, who hadn't finished his argument with Officer Stevens yet, turned on Colonel Bender. "If I was the type to hide lobsters, they wouldn't be where any badge could find them."

"Don't get cute with us," Officer Stevens said, his voice raised and carrying a hint of anger. He gave Tucker his license back and plucked the driver's license from James's hand. "James *Morrow*... probably a stretch, but are you related to Detective Maya Morrow?"

*What's that probably a stretch bullshit?* "Maya's my wife."

Officer Stevens stopped writing, and his eyebrows jumped up. "Huh, no shit." He clicked his pen several times. "You ought to know better." He wrote out the rest of the ticket.

Tucker turned on Officer Stevens. "Give him a damn break."

He ignored Tucker and handed James the ticket.

James slid the paper into his pocket. "Tucker, hey, don't worry about it..."

Tucker swung his flushed face in James's direction. He raised his palms and stepped backward. *This is what Tucker's like when he's angry.* An image of Kevin cowering under that rage popped into James's head. Or was his anger justifiable? *These officers aren't exactly friendly guys.*

Colonel Bender pulled out a lobster and spread its tail. He brandished the lobster tail inches from Tucker's flaring nostrils. "You see that? This one's notched."

Tucker's mouth hung open. "Are you insane? That's a crack in the tail—doesn't even have a shape to it!"

Colonel Bender ignored Tucker's protests and brandished a pad of his own.

Tucker's voice shifted to a mocking tone. "Couple of big tough guys here, eh?" He stabbed his thumb into his chest. "I've been lobstering since I could walk. I know a notch when I see one."

"There's really no point in arguing." Colonel Bender snapped a picture of the lobster then cut the bands before he set it free in the channel.

"What the hell is this really about?" Tucker said, digging his fists into his hips.

Colonel Bender handed Tucker a pink piece of paper. "We're trying to stop poachers. Even you should be able to understand that. You'll want to be more careful with your catch, Mr. Flynn. We set the rules and regs for a reason, you know." He stepped back over onto their boat with Officer Stevens.

Tucker tore the paper in half and let the pieces fall to the wet deck. "I'm going to fight this! That was not notched!"

The officers offered toothless, melancholy smiles as they pushed their boat away from the *Periwinkle*. Tucker stormed into the wheelhouse; he spit over the railing as the marine patrol boat drifted away. When Tucker regained his composure, he apologized to James for the ticket and promised to pay for it somehow.

James shrugged. "I was driving without a boating license. You didn't force me. Plus my wife's a detective. She'll take care of the ticket."

"It ain't right. Those guys... just ain't right."

"Do they stop you often?"

"Marine patrol is always prowling around. They check to make sure you have enough life vests, or lights, or some stupid shit, but I've never seen them with a Fish and Game guy on their boat like that."

James shook his head. "Doesn't make it any easier on you."

Tucker shifted his hat. Frown marks sprouted between his eyes. James would bet Tucker was still arguing with them in his head. He had a temper. What he did with that fire was the question. James pictured Kevin bringing home a bad report card and Tucker ripping it in half as he'd done the ticket. Kevin's lips trembling, tears falling from his glassy blue eyes, and his hands covering his mouth, his face shrinking under Tucker's glare. What would a man with a short fuse do under the cover of his own roof?

Back at the dock, they tied off the *Periwinkle*. Tucker hosed her down and stowed all the gear in the darkness of the hold. He waved at an attractive woman with sharp features. The woman sauntered across the dock toward Tucker the way an outdoor cat would. She patted her brown hair, tied back in a messy bun, laced with small spindling curls that ached to be sprung loose. When she stopped beside James, she took a long drag from her stubby cigarette.

Tucker set down the buckets of lobsters. "James, this is my wife, Melanie."

"Nice to meet you," James said.

She carried the stale scent of cigarettes. Even with crow's feet stamped under her eyes, she radiated a stubborn vitality. "Likewise." She shot smoke out the side of her mouth. "Looks like Tuck worked you to the bone today."

James hadn't thought about his appearance. His T-shirt and cargo shorts were soaked, covered in fish guts and green algae stains. He smelled like seaweed and mackerel. "I'll have some good blisters tomorrow."

Her knowing smile came with a soft laugh. "Did he invite you for supper?"

"He didn't. I would be happy to come if you'd have me." Maya would definitely wonder where he was. "But I should let my wife know first."

She nodded and cleared her throat again. Her fist covered her mouth, and her silver bracelets made clinking noises. "Tell her to come over for dinner too."

No reason not to invite her. In fact, he was eager to introduce Maya to the Flynns. They could both use some potential friends who weren't cops or social workers. "All right, I will."

# CHAPTER 5

MAYA STROLLED THROUGH THE RACKS at the thrift store, her hands rubbing polyester dresses, worn corduroy pants, and rows of faded jeans. She breathed in the mix of moth balls, detergent, and air freshener. James couldn't stand the smell in these places, which was fine because Goodwill was her thinking place. Many nights after work, she'd go there to turn a tag or just wander through tired suit jackets of every shade.

Two women in their fifties convened over a pair of pants in the next aisle. "Do you think these would fit John? I love the fabric."

The other woman purred, "That's a great price."

Maya sighed then hummed her mother's favorite jazz tune, "Black Coffee" by Ella Fitzgerald. The Vasquez brothers' stash house raid — what a fiasco. The town's residents had to be happy with a drug bust of that size, even if it wasn't heroin.

Wade had put his internal affairs hat on and run her through interviews. He'd slipped her a couple of winks, like the good old boy he was, and she answered his questions and fulfilled her duty. Her lawyer, a mild-mannered man with a pathetic comb-over, was Dan Whitley, and he'd done plenty of behind-the-scenes work to prove her innocence. In his office, he'd explained that since there was only one side of the story and the only living witnesses were cops, all lights ahead appeared green.

Then she'd had the mandatory psychiatric visit with Carol Wayneright. What an unexpected delight she'd turned out to be. Maya smiled, thinking of the energetic middle-aged psychiatrist she'd talked with yesterday. Despite what the chief had said, Maya was going back to work tomorrow. The required three days were up, and it was time to get back to work. Time to find the heroin traffickers.

"Oh, that's cute. You have a little girl at home, darling?" the old woman beside her said with a southern accent. Her thin white hair was cinched by a silver hair clip. A hunched back and slanted neck forced her pupils to float up to achieve eye contact.

Maya had been holding a pink onesie. "No, not yet." After three months of trying, all they had to show for it was a growing pile of negative pregnancy tests. Maya gave the woman a generous smile.

The woman's red square-cut fingernails flashed as she batted the air. "Oh, you should, honey, they're little angels. I never thought I could love anything more than my husband, Chester, until I had my three little ones." The woman touched Maya's shoulder as she shuffled down the aisle.

Maya's phone went off in her pocket. James asked her to come to dinner with his two new friends. She agreed and jotted down the address on a piece of scrap paper from her pocketbook. After she hung up, she reexamined the pink onesie. She imagined a crying, chubby baby girl filling the outfit. She'd hold her close, sharing one heartbeat, and hush her cries.

# CHAPTER 6

T HE FLYNNS LIVED IN A humble one-story cottage halfway down a narrow, dead-end street. Kevin was shooting a basketball through a rusted hoop that hung over the driveway when they arrived. Tucker's beat-up truck was resting in the garage.

James high-fived Kevin, who showcased his crooked bucktooth grin. As Melanie passed her son, she kissed his forehead and Tucker tousled his hair. Kevin's smile appeared genuine, and he didn't come across as timid toward his parents. *Maybe I'm just being paranoid with this bruise thing.* Kids got bruises, especially active kids. Boys beat each other up. *I would know. I got in my fair share of fights as a kid.*

James followed Melanie inside then removed his squishy sneakers and soggy socks.

Melanie ducked into a bedroom and came back with a handful of folded sweats and a fresh pair of balled socks. "Here, these are Tuck's."

He thanked her, and she waved him toward the bathroom. A big conch shell sat atop the toilet tank lid, and other shells, dried lobster claws, and bits of coral littered the counters. James stripped and put on the dry clothes, taking a moment to massage the tender red skin on his leg where the lobster trap rope had squeezed him.

He left his damp clothes in the bathroom and walked out into the living room. Tucker and Melanie talked through a clattering of pots and pans. The worn polyester couch and blue La-Z-Boy chair orbited a wooden lobster trap coffee table that dominated the room. Along the right wall, a cuckoo clock ticked away. He stepped off the wood floor and onto the thin, tan carpet of a solarium, the surrounding windows covered with yellow film and a layer of dust. A collection of old chairs and a battered antique love seat made a cramped semi-circle around the antique television, topped by rabbit ear antenna. A stack of board games sat on a three-tiered shelf. He walked over to the boxes and saw a sad face drawn into dust on top of Mouse Trap.

Kevin came in from outside and plopped himself sideways on a chair in the solarium, his legs dangling over one of the arms. "What's going on, Mr. Jay?"

"Not much, Kevin." James glanced past the living room to the kitchen, where Melanie and Tucker were preparing food. James sat on the loveseat. He leaned closer to Kevin. "Hey, did you ever tell your parents about those bruises on your arms and legs?"

"From the bully?"

"Yeah." His story hadn't changed.

"I told my dad." Kevin scratched the chair's fabric.

"And what did he do?"

"He went to the bully's house and talked to his dad."

James nodded. Maybe it was just a bully situation. *Still, I have to dig deeper, and Kevin seems willing to talk.* "Is the bully giving you any more problems?"

"Nope. Look, my skin's already healed. I'm a quick healer."

*I need to know.* James hesitated then said, "Did your mom or dad ever give you any bruises?"

"What? No, why?" Kevin tilted his head and frowned.

That confused face was all he needed to see. They weren't abusing him. James put up his hands. "Oh, I just want to make sure."

"They yell sometimes, but my dad is a good dad."

"And your mom?"

"She's the best mom in the whole wide world, except when she makes me eat green beans. I hate green beans." Kevin stuck out his tongue.

*Time to patch up and deflect.* "I think your parents are

great too. Your dad took me out on his boat today. It was wicked awesome."

Kevin sat up straight in his chair. "You guys catch any fish?"

"We did."

Kevin smiled. "That's my favorite. I like fishing for mackerel the most. My record is two hundred twelve mackerel."

They talked about fishing some more, then Kevin went to his room.

"I'm glad to see you're a Patriots fan." Tucker's booming voice broke the silence, startling James.

"Holy crap!"

Tucker chuckled.

James took a second to recover then glanced at his borrowed sweat shirt. The red, white, and blue logo was streaked across his own chest.

"I never asked you, do you even like lobster?" Tucker asked.

"I do, although I haven't had lobster in years, so you might have to refresh me on how to eat one."

"No problem. I threw your wet clothes in the wash, by the way."

In the kitchen, a large pot was on the stove. The lobsters were crawling on the kitchen table, each releasing frothy bubbles from their mouths. James and Tucker sat across from each other in the living room, the lobster trap coffee table between them.

James eyed the massive loadbearing beam above the coffee table. "You said this was your parents' place, right? Seems like they left you a great house."

"Thanks, we love it here. I'm not one of those guys who needs much. Being close to the sea is all I want. That's why we're so stressed about this foreclosure crap." Tucker sighed and ran his hands through his hair.

"When did your parents pass away?"

"My dad died seven years back. My mom—she loved my father—let herself go after Dad left us, and we buried her alongside him six months later. Don't ask me why, but Dad never believed in life insurance, and his and mom's funerals

50

came out of our pocket." He bowed his head for a moment then continued. "My dad had always been a proud man, but a poor man at that. When I saw how much he was in the hole on the house, I knew I was balls deep in the muck. At this point, we owe more than the house is worth. The leeches at the bank know we're in over our heads, hence the foreclosure notice." He licked his lips. "Together, me and Melanie don't make enough. It's hard enough keeping food in the fridge."

"Lobstering is your only job, I take it?" James crossed his legs.

"As of a couple months ago, yeah, it is. I've done boat and engine repair for ten years, but my boss canned me. Guy says he can't afford to have an unlicensed tech on staff this year. Now all I got is the lobsters, and once it gets too cold and the lobsters head out to deeper water, I won't even have that." Tucker rubbed his furrowed brow as if he were trying to rub off a stain. "If that ain't enough, the prices of lobsters dropped by more than half this summer, and fuel prices are through the roof. Plus Fish and Game has a stick up their ass and puts on more and more regulations that I got to pay for." Tucker shook his head. "Thank God for Melanie. She's working her ass off waiting tables," Tucker said loud enough so Melanie could hear.

Melanie appeared from the kitchen and sat on the arm of Tucker's chair. She massaged her foot in a way that another person would unconsciously stroke their chin. "We've had a bad luck streak running for a while now." She switched to the other foot.

"I mean, there are plenty of other people worse off," Tucker said. "But right now, we're just kind of... stuck." Tucker crossed his thick forearms. The fork-like artery in his forearm wrapped around the muscle like a length of parachute cord.

"Which bank is your mortgage through?" James asked Tucker.

"Coastal Light Bank."

James eyed his own hands. *Who do I know that works for that bank? Kathy.* "I know a manager at that bank. She and I exchange favors from time to time. I'll call her tomorrow and see if she can offer some sort of extension for the time being. I mean, worth a try, right?"

Melanie's hands were folded together as if she were praying. Her face reflected a sudden relief, as if she'd been under water and holding her breath. Tucker chewed his bottom lip with his front teeth.

"More time is exactly what we need," Melanie said.

James nodded. What next? Tucker needed another job clearly. "What kind of jobs are you looking for?"

Tucker tilted his neck to the right then the left, not stopping until his bones cracked. "I do odd jobs and landscaping sometimes, but I don't really have any other skills aside from boat engines and fiberglass work." His round shoulders sunk.

James glanced at his borrowed clothes. "I have a contact at a security company." He let the statement sink in for a moment. "He's always needs reliable workers. The best part is they have all sorts of shifts."

Melanie, who'd been bobbing her head, stopped and spoke to Tucker. "Not like it would be hard labor, Tuck, and you could take my car since your truck is broken down right now. I wouldn't need the car if you worked nights."

Tucker uncrossed his arms and rubbed his knees. James wished he could read his thoughts.

Finally Tucker broke his silence. "Yeah, I'm interested."

James relaxed his jaw. "Great, I'll call him tomorrow and put you two in touch."

They all turned as the cuckoo bird flew out of its tiny yellow door. Eight o'clock.

James tossed his right leg over the left. "Just don't overexert yourselves. I've seen too many people work too hard to get by, and that puts a strain on the family. I'm sure you know that kids are affected by financial troubles too."

"That's why we got Kevin involved in the rec center," Tucker said. "He loves basketball. His older brother, Jacob, loved it too. I ain't Sigmund Freud, but I think it's Kevin's way of keeping his big brother alive."

"Kevin looked up to Jacob so much," Melanie added weakly. Her eyelids became twin dams.

Tucker put a hand on her shoulder and rubbed her back. James was a stranger to their intimate sorrow, which made him feel a pang of discomfort. Melanie sniffed and wiped her eyes. The dams held.

A clanging pot lid, accompanied by the hiss of spilling water, in the kitchen broke the mood.

"Oops! Boiling over. I'll put the lobsters in." Melanie dried her eyes on her shirt sleeves as she fled the room.

Tucker and James stepped into the kitchen to watch the action. Melanie's mitted hand lifted the cover, releasing steam that rose in a rush of heat, hitting the ceiling and spreading like the arms of an octopus. James regarded the banded lobsters on the table, moving as slow as a herd of tortoises. Melanie scooped them up one by one, and before the creatures could realize, they were hanging over the metal rim of a bubbling hot spring. They lifted their claws in protest, but it was too late. The last lobster went in on top of his brothers and reached out for the light as the lid was slid over his stainless steel tomb. The pot shook, and Melanie held the lid down for a few moments.

A short time later, the cover was lifted and the bright Mars-red crustaceans were revealed. Tucker microwaved some butter and set the table. Tucker offered James a beer, but James turned him down.

"Not a beer guy?" Tucker asked.

"Alcohol and my blood don't mix. My dad had a drinking problem. I try not to mess with the stuff."

"Was he a social worker like you?" Melanie asked.

"A manager at a fish cannery, when he wasn't drunk or slugging my mom and me." James hadn't meant to say the last part; it just slid out, as if he were singing the last few lyrics of a song on the radio. James scratched his hairline. "Sorry, I must be tired from lugging all those lobster traps. My dad had his problems."

Tucker took a long drink of his beer.

James continued. "I do like my job though. There's so much awfulness out there, you know? As cliché as it sounds, I believe somebody has to fight the good fight."

"You're a better man than most," Melanie said, eying Tucker.

When Maya arrived, James introduced her to the Flynn family. Melanie called for Kevin and beckoned them all to take their seats at the table.

The table was littered with food: whole lobsters, lobster rolls, lobster stew, mashed potatoes, and vegetables. Kevin, who claimed he didn't like the taste of lobster, ate some fish sticks and a Mountain Dew. Tucker threw back several beers. There was no shortage of laughter and smiles.

As Maya probed for more meat in her lobster, she said, "Tucker, I hear there are territories on the water. Trap wars. Is that true?"

"There can be, to some extent. I mean, some guys who've been laying traps their whole lives would be pretty steamed if some new guy came in and plopped his traps on top of theirs." His thick arms tangled in the air to show the effect. "Hell, people tangle their gear in mine every now and then. I try to save their lines if I can. I'm not the oldest dog out there, but my dad kind of grandfathered me into the business. Folks remember him and give me more slack. I know just about every guy out there fishing." He bit off a mouthful of lobster roll and spoke through his bites. "I'm not out there to be a dick, you understand. I just try to cover some territory before the season's over and the lobsters move back into deeper water."

Maya ripped off her lobster's leg and sucked the meat out as if it were a straw. She dabbed her lips with a napkin and turned to Tucker. "I remember hearing a story about one lobsterman who got so angry he took a shotgun to another guy's motor. Was that last year or the year before?"

"Last summer," Tucker said, putting down the lobster roll.

"You ever seen anything like that?" she asked.

He picked his teeth with a fingernail. "Not really. I steer away from trouble and don't cross the ornery guys."

Maya sprinkled some pepper on her mashed potatoes. "Have you ever seen anything *suspicious* going on in the harbor?"

"What do you mean?" Tucker stopped cleaning his teeth and set down the beer that had been glued to his hand for most of the evening.

"Oh, I don't know. Noticed anything out of the ordinary at the docks? New faces? Shady business?"

"Can't say I have."

"Nothing at all?"

Tucker looked at James with a smile. "Am I under arrest?" He offered his wrists to Maya and laughed.

James came to Tucker's aid. "I know, seriously, Maya. He said he hasn't seen anything."

"Excuse me," Melanie said and left the room.

Maya took a bite of the potatoes. "I'm *only* asking. Never hurts to have a man on the inside."

Tucker went back to attending his beer. He scratched the back of his head. "I can't say I've seen much worth talking about. If I do, I'll be sure to let you know."

"See?" Maya pointed at James. "That's how crimes are solved. The public usually knows more than we do."

"Makes sense," James said.

Melanie came back with a glass of water.

"We're going to take you two and Kevin out to dinner next," Maya said in a cheerful tone.

"Sounds like a plan." Tucker got up and retrieved another beer.

The couples talked, laughed, and exchanged stories under the glow of the kitchen light long after Kevin went to bed. When Tucker and Melanie started clearing dishes, James faced Maya and walked his fingers on the table. Maya nodded, and they said their good-byes.

When they were back home and lying in bed, James kissed Maya and thanked her for coming to dinner. He'd handed her the marine patrol's ticket before they got in bed, and she'd rolled her eyes and taken the ticket.

"They were really nice, but I thought you said they were clients or something?"

He rubbed his forehead. "No, I cried wolf. Thought they might be hitting Kevin—furthest thing from the truth. They're great parents."

"You're a crazy person, Jamesey. I didn't get that domestic violence vibe at all."

James threw up his hands. "Like I said, I must be getting paranoid."

"I'm glad you invited me though, because it got me thinking."

James rubbed her shoulder. "About what?"

Maya rubbed her jaw with her thumb. "Maybe the heroin isn't being trafficked by land. Maybe it's coming in from the sea?"

# CHAPTER 7

MAYA WATCHED THE FISHERMEN SPRAY off their boats with garden hoses. Blood and entrails slid off the decks and poured into the water below. Sea gulls dove after the floating bits of pulpy flesh. The deckhands, consumed with finishing their job before the sun fell any lower in the sky, didn't seem to notice the birds fighting. Her mandatory three days off were up, and she was relieved to be back to work. An active police presence monitored the piers and shipping wharves, but no one checked the smaller marinas and boat docks. She'd spoken with a few fishermen who'd been willing to exchange small talk with her, but none of them gave her anything worth her time. Most avoided her gaze, throwing themselves into their work or vanishing below at the sound of her steps. Those were the ones she wanted to talk to, the ones who didn't want to talk to her.

She walked to the end of a skinny dock and examined the murky water and the clay-brown sand below. Her index finger touched the dock post to her right, and she dragged it over the dark-green slime clinging to the moist wood. Tiny, tightly sealed blue mussels clung to the post in clusters. She breathed in and smelled the sun-cooked algae and baking wood. A puff of air shot out of the side of her mouth, tossing her loose bangs off her eyebrows.

A lobster boat passed underneath a short bridge nearby. The overweight captain spoke over his shoulder to the two men standing idle about the deck. They seemed indifferent to his barked orders. She locked eyes with the man leaning against the back of the boat. His complexion was tan, like finished wood, and his features were nearly onyx. He wore a clean red-and-white netted hat that Maya couldn't imagine was his own, as it hadn't been broken in at all. The man's intense gaze pressed down on her, as if measuring her worth, while his stance appeared casual.

She felt footsteps approaching her from behind, and without turning around, she gleaned what she could. A slow, steady gait—not heavy. The way the weight of the feet shifted on the wood suggested shoes, not the white or yellow boots the fishermen wore. Purposeful steps coming right for her.

"Afternoon, Detective."

She turned around slowly to face a man with a wide-brimmed tan hat, mirror-aviator sunglasses, a forest-green uniform shirt, and army-green ironed pants. "Afternoon."

He offered a toothy smile. "I hope I didn't scare you."

She noted the badge pinned to his chest. "Not at all, Colonel... Bender."

He looked at his name tag and back at her. "Sometimes I forget we wear these."

She didn't know many Fish and Game officers. "Have we met before?"

"Not formally. I did catch you on TV this weekend though. Nice job tossing that Vasquez prick to the ground." He offered her his hand, and she accepted it.

"Yeah, it got a little ugly."

"It's good. Will show the rest of the dealers what happens when they fuck with the cops." He had a sharp smile and a bushy cherry-blond mustache. "So I saw your squad car parked in the lot and was interested to see what brings you to my meager beat."

"The view isn't a good enough reason?" she asked, nodding at the shimmering water.

He stepped closer, carrying the scent of peppermint. "There are far prettier and less stinky views than this stretch. I can show you one if you have time."

"Maybe another day." He seemed friendly enough, if not a touch overbearing.

"Course, some do find the dock and fishermen appealing, but me, I try not to mingle. Makes it harder when I have to hand out fines."

"I get that." Maya glanced at the lobster boat steering toward the main channel of the Skog, no doubt heading toward the ocean. Seemed odd that everyone else was heading into harbor for the night and that boat was leaving. She squinted to read the name painted across the boat's backside. "You know that boat, Colonel?"

"That one?" Colonel Bender stepped beside her. The peppermint scent overpowered all of the other smells close by. "That there's the *Water Angel*, Tom Braxton's vessel. Why?"

"Just wondering."

Colonel Bender lowered his sunglasses, revealing slate blue eyes. He raised his eyebrows at her as if to say, *What are you up to, lady*?

"Have you encountered any drug activity on your 'meager beat'?"

He was quick to give her another smile then spoke in slow words. "In all my fifteen years of working on land, dock, and sea, I can say I've bagged and tagged everything *but* drugs, Detective." His nostrils flared.

"You can just call me Maya."

At six and a half feet tall, he stood a foot above Maya, and his hat cast a shadow over her. She wanted to step back, as he was only a foot away from her, but she was running out of dock.

"Maya," he said.

"Well, I've got to get back to *my* beat." She slid around him. "Thanks for the time."

"Don't mention it."

Maya walked away from him. In her car, she saw him staring out at the water the way she had. Perhaps trying to understand what had mesmerized her? Maybe his job was pretty slow? Maya didn't know much about how Fish and Game operated, but she did know body language. Maybe it was just her being who she was, but she'd definitely noticed his nostrils open to suck up more air after he'd claimed he'd never encountered drugs. The human body almost always spoke the truth even when the mouth lied.

# CHAPTER 8

J AMES DIDN'T DARE LOOK AWAY from the glacial-blue eyes of
the man a half-step away from giving into gravity and 125
feet of open air. Far below the bridge and the man's boot
heels, the outgoing tide was visible; one of the world's fastest
currents pulled water out to sea as if someone had yanked the
plug from the ocean's drain. A tractor trailer truck, switching
lanes to avoid the parked maroon Dodge Ram pickup in the
middle of the bridge, drove past. The horn blasts shook James
as hard as the rush of air that trailed the truck. James blinked
and stepped closer to the man, who pulled back and took one
of his hands off the rail, leaving behind a wet handprint on the
green steel.

"Hey, I just want to talk," James said.

"Stay back!"

James lifted his arms above his head and offered his palms.
"Listen, man, I'm not a cop. I'm just a social worker—a normal
guy like you. I want to help, that's all."

"I don't need your help. It's over. I'm going to do it!" The
man's veins appeared like cracks across his neck.

James swallowed in an effort to wet his dry throat. Today
had been the type of weather New Englanders talked about
all winter—a shorts-and-flip-flops kind of day. James had
taken his moped for a long ride after work. He'd just wanted
a chance to absorb the last of the sun and let the wind peel
away his thoughts. He could have driven right past the truck
parked in the middle of the Skog River Bridge, part of I-95. No
one would've blamed him for assuming the owner was simply

waiting for a tow. Instead, James had slowed down enough to catch the expression of the man stepping over the rail. He had communicated more to James in his frozen stare than words could have. It wasn't the first time a jumper had stood on that bridge.

The man's tousled hair flailed with the wind, and the bridge shook underfoot as cars rushed by on either side. In the moments when no cars passed, James could hear the man's rapid breathing.

"Listen, my name's James, James Morrow. What's your name, buddy?"

"Carl. Listen, when the cops come here, you tell them it was Carl Mending who jumped today. That'll save them the trouble."

"What do you do, Carl?"

"I'm a — I mean, I *was*... a fisherman. Now I got nothing."

James winced. "You have any family, Carl?" James held his breath.

Carl breathed a gulp of air then released a shaky exhale. "Got a wife and two kids." He glanced at the dark-blue water as a tugboat chugged upriver against the outgoing current. Carl switched hands on the rail.

James exhaled and tilted his head sideways. "So what are you doing this for, huh? You can step back over that rail now, get into your truck, and drive back to your family like this never happened. I won't say a thing, Carl."

"I'm doing this *for* my family."

A car sped by. Rock music blared for a moment, then it was gone. James dropped his hand by his side and stepped forward.

"Hey —" Carl leaned backward, still holding on by one hand.

James moved as if he were stepping through tide pools with bare feet. "I just don't want to get hit, Carl. I'm going to get out of the road here but to the left of you there." James pointed farther down the rail.

Carl's red-ringed eyes followed James. Carl's cheeks were wind-burnt, his mouth was flat, and he had a gray unshaven jawline that matched his salt-and-pepper shaggy hair.

The sudden whine of police sirens came from both ends of the bridge.

Carl's eyes darted left and right, then he frowned as he shook his head. "That's that." Carl peeked over his shoulder at the river again.

"Carl, my wife's a cop. We can get through this. This isn't that bad, man. Not even a problem, really."

"This is bigger than you and me, James." Carl's voice seemed steadier, and he spoke as if his own words deflated him.

The police blocked off the bridge traffic on both sides. Several cruisers parked thirty yards away. Uniformed officers and detectives in suits walked over to James and Carl.

James put his hands in front of him as if he were grasping an invisible ball and said, "Listen, we all have our bad days. My day was garbage. I had to hear about how a baby was living in hellish conditions while the parents were shooting up downstairs." James concentrated on holding Carl's gaze. "But at the end of the day, we have to let that crap go." James's eyes opened wide when he realized his word choice. He quickly continued. "This is—"

"Heroin?" Carl leaned forward and put both of his hands on the rail.

"Excuse me?" James put a hand to his ear. The red-and-blue lights flashing in his peripheral vision distracted him. He heard the idling engines of the squad cars.

A man cleared his throat several feet behind James. "Hey, guys, I'm Detective Wade Copley. How we doing?"

Carl didn't take his eyes off James. The dark crevasses of his irises glowed with a pale blue light. "Were they shooting up heroin?"

"Yeah, they had problems, Carl, way worse than you or me."

Wade stepped closer to the rail between James and Carl. "Let's just calm down here, boys, and try to sort this out." Wade straightened his belt and tossed his gum from one side of his mouth to the other as he spoke.

James felt a hand on his back and turned around so fast

his neck cracked. He exhaled when he saw Maya. Her brow momentarily furrowed then her dark skin smoothed over. James made himself smile.

"Hey, Carl, let me introduce you to my wife here," James said. "Maya, this is Carl Mending. He was a fisherman. Carl's got a wife and two kids." James stepped backward and ushered Maya in front of him.

Carl eyed Wade, who'd steadily been inching closer.

"Nice to meet you, Carl. I'm Detective Maya Morrow. I work for Newborough Police Department. I just want to talk. Is that okay with you?" Her voice was soft.

Carl snapped at Wade, "Hey, back up, I'm serious!"

Maya put her hand up as if to pat the air. "Okay, okay, no problem, Wade'll back up. Wade! Do it!" Maya's eyebrows shot up.

Wade hesitated then retreated two steps.

"Okay, no problem. We're just here to talk," Maya said.

Carl's raised voice dripped with acid. "Everyone just wants to talk. Well, I don't want to talk to cops, how about that? You're all a bunch of corrupt hired guns."

"Who would you like to talk to?" Maya asked.

James backed away until he fell behind the line of uniformed policemen. He heard someone speak into a radio and say, "Marine Patrol boats are getting into place below."

"James, hey, over here," Sam's deep voice broke the air. "Come with me to the barricade. Maya wants you to back away from this. Don't worry, this thing"—Sam pointed in Carl's direction—"could take a while. Most of these guys are up there for hours."

James followed Sam to his black unmarked car on the downtown Newborough side of the bridge. He was in his thirties, like James, and just over six feet tall as well. Sam's dark hair was shaved short, and like his fellow detectives, he wore a dark suit and tie with a badge dangling from a chain around his neck. When they got to the car, Sam pulled out a worn black moleskin notebook just shy of the size of a legal pad and a silver pen flipped between his fingers.

He leafed through several pages and stopped when he got to a clean page.

Sam cleared his throat. "How did you come upon this jumper?" He wrote 6/20/2014 on the top and added the time of 7:58 p.m.

"Drove by and saw him stepping over the rail." James leaned against Sam's black Crown Victoria. The sun sank into the headwaters of the Skog River, unfolding shadows across the trees and the distant docks. From his end of the bridge, James could still make out Carl, Wade, and Maya.

"Sorry about this crap, man. I'm going to need you to detail it all out for me. Reports and necessary info..."

James regurgitated his short conversation with the suicidal out-of-work fisherman. Sam jotted brief notes. When Sam stopped his inquiry to talk on the radio, James stared at the braided channel of the Skog River as it spilled into Newborough Harbor. On one side of the river lay downtown—red brick buildings and plump wooden clapboard colonials with dark-blue shingles built along the water. Timber docks stood fast, holding roped-off white fiberglass pleasure boats. Fire-engine-red tugs with black smoke stacks bobbed in the river. James followed an emerald-green car crawling through a narrow corridor like a June bug.

On the opposite side of the Skog, Newborough was broken into suburbs until the land dropped in elevation and turned into protected marshland followed by several miles of pristine beaches. Newborough was wedged between the coastal towns of Rye to the north and North Hampton to the south. The Skog River, which cut the town in half, offered a small shipping port that wasn't quite as big as Portsmouth to the north.

"See Chief McCourt over there?" Sam pointed at the mustached, stocky man in his fifties, standing behind a squad car and watching with folded arms. "He wants Wade to talk this guy down." Sam chuckled. "Wade's pretty good at that — talking."

The orange-and-purple ribbons of the sunset unfolded in the hills across the west.

"Sometimes I wonder if there are any normal people left out there," James said.

"Me too." Sam poked James in the shoulder. "Ha, we're not too sane ourselves. Normal people wouldn't be shooting the shit while watching a poor son of a bitch contemplating swan-diving into the Skog."

James shrugged and gazed at Sam.

Sam sighed then joined James in leaning against the car. He crossed his arms. "Listen, why don't you — oh, shit!" Sam's eyes went wide.

Carl was shouting. Maya and Wade protested, then Carl's hands lifted from the railing and he fell backward with a long, hollow scream. The police rushed to the side of the bridge. The scream cut off abruptly.

"No," James whispered.

Carl couldn't have survived the fall, not from that height. James rushed to the side of the bridge and stared at the dark-blue water, ripples, and white foam. Could he have stopped it? He should have grabbed Carl and tried to pull him over. Several boats converged where he'd hit the water. *Why, Carl?*

Sam shook his head and muttered, "Damn it. Sorry bastard."

When James caught up with Maya, she was shaking her head, as was Wade. All the cops were shaking their heads as if they were trying to erase the image of Carl from their memories.

# CHAPTER 9

JAMES STEPPED INTO THE MONROE Recreational Center at five forty-five in the evening. After a weekend spent trying to forget Carl Mending's suicide, he'd been eagerly awaiting his time with the kids to make some fresh memories and just laugh. After finishing typing out a long report at work, he'd left the office later than usual and hadn't thought to change into his gym clothes. He walked through the court. The boys were clustered together in the center, and stray basketballs lay abandoned as if they were balloons after a party. The boys' hushed chattering seemed odd. James didn't see any staffers around. He witnessed several unmistakable frowns of concern sprout amid the group. He acknowledged them with a dead wave.

The restroom was in a small hallway right off the basketball court. James pushed open the mold-colored door and stepped inside. The walls were covered in thousands of square-inch white porcelain tiles that, over the years, had cracked and yellowed. Even the urinals were lined with tiled skin, like the scales of a massive snake. James heard a shuffling of feet in one of the stalls. He went into the big handicap one, unzipped his duffel bag, and pulled out his gym clothes.

More movement erupted, and a body pushed against the dividing wall, accompanied by a hushed voice. "Shit."

A small object hit the ground and skittered into James's stall. He stared at the wicked-looking syringe. The small plastic plunger had been pushed all the way to the bottom. The black lines striping the side indicated it could hold five milliliters.

Underneath the plastic was a brown film, left over residue. The needle had an ugly, cold, metallic shine.

James instinctively kicked the vicious-looking instrument and watched it settle in the farthest corner of his stall, blending into ages of dirt and shadows. He ducked his head and saw two sets of sneakers in the next stall.

James froze. Maybe the syringe was for insulin? The thought felt as false as wooden teeth, but he held on to the idea as he stepped out of his stall and knocked on the door of the next one over. He aimed for the correct level of authority. "I saw the needle. Open up, boys."

"Hey, man," a boy said, desperation shaking his voice. "That thing was already on the ground when we—I mean, I got in here. I was just kicking it out of my stall."

James knew the kid wanted James to go away, and James wished he could. He'd already pictured the consequences lining up in his head. "Open up. This is the last time I'm going to tell you."

"I'm shitting, man. I'm shitting! Don't come in here. Oh, fuck!" The voice changed from aggravation to surprise as a body hit the floor as if someone had dropped a heavy piece of prime rib onto a stone cutting board.

James heard a sickening crack of bone meeting hard tile. Derek Fanning's face lay motionless and slack on the ground, blood oozing from his mouth.

James pounded on the stall door. "Open this door right now! He's hurt!" Anger and adrenaline burned through him like fire through a gas line.

The lock slid, and the green door folded inward. James made a quick assessment. The redheaded teenager inside was trying to lift Derek's limp body from the floor. On the toilet tank lid was an open black bag with needles, cotton filters, a spoon, red lighter, and a small lump of brown powder wrapped in plastic. James grabbed the teenager by the wrist and hauled him out of the stall. The kid's hands were shaking, and his freckled face went white as he tried explaining, but he stumbled over his own tongue. James hadn't seen him around the center before.

"Go get another adult in here fast," James said.

He nodded and ran out of the bathroom. James slid out his cell phone, dialed 9-1-1, and pressed the speaker button. He grabbed Derek by the shirt and rolled him onto his back. He was limp and showed no signs of life. James grabbed his collar and dragged him out of the stall into a clear patch of floor. James heard the phone ring over the speaker.

"9-1-1 dispatch, what is your emergency?"

"Listen, I'm at the Monroe Recreational Center in Newborough, New Hampshire. I've got a kid, a boy, I think he's fifteen. He's unconscious. I think he overdosed."

The dispatch woman's voice came alive. "The Monroe Recreational Center, yes, I'm sending emergency personnel there immediately. Please stay on the line, sir. Can you tell me if he's breathing or has a pulse?" Her question echoed off the tiles.

James moved Derek's long, scrubby hair out of his face and put his cheek next to the Derek's bloody mouth. The mandatory CPR training he'd taken in the office was slowly coming back to him. He put his fingers on the boy's neck. He jabbed his fingers around, feeling nothing but clammy lifeless skin.

"Sir, is he breathing?" the dispatcher asked.

"No, he isn't breathing, and I have no, well, I'm pretty sure there's no pulse. Should I do CPR?" James asked.

"Yes, I'll talk you through it. Give him one hundred chest compressions per minute.

The beat of 'Stayin' Alive' is a perfect match if that helps."

James found the right spot on Derek's chest, clasped his hands, and counted out loud with every compression. "One, two, three, four..."

Derek's lips had become a splotchy blue color. The same color was taking over his face.

"The police and ambulance are both on their way. Keep

giving him chest compressions until he shows signs of life or medical personnel relieve you. They'll be there soon."

James continued giving the compressions, aware that the door had opened behind him.

Brian slid to his knees beside him. "Jesus Christ! What the hell happened?"

James didn't answer him, too afraid to lose count.

Derek's ripped jeans were rolled up at the bottoms. He wore gray Converse sneakers that shook every time James pushed down on his chest.

James yelled at the phone, "When is that ambulance going to get here?"

The voice on the phone resurfaced. "They're three minutes out."

"I'll go show them how to get in here," Brian said and took off running.

James pumped Derek's chest hard. A crack and a pop shuddered across Derek's chest, and a broken rib bone flailed under James's palm. He hesitated and asked, "I think I broke his rib. What should I do?"

The dispatcher responded, "Continue chest compressions."

James resumed compressions. The bathroom was silent except for the desperate sounds of James's efforts. He tried to work up a prayer, but nothing came to him. *Any second now, he's going to cough and snap out of it, just like in the movies. Come on, come on, come on!*

It was as if he were pressing down on a lifeless fish. The tiles dug hard into James's knees; he felt his arms tire and grow heavy. He was losing the battle, yet he struggled on. "Damn it! Derek, you can't die. I won't let you!"

James heard shoes thrum across the court. He pushed harder, trying to get Derek's heart to stir. His long hair was parted down the middle and fell backward limply. Derek's cold face was peaceful, as if he were sleeping in the snow. Trace freckles were stamped under his eyes and over the bridge of his nose.

Dark blood seeped out of the hole in his left forearm, tainted with something evil that was polluting his young, fragile body.

"Derek, I need you to wake up. Please," James said.

"In here. He's in here!"

Blue-uniformed paramedics funneled through the door with a uniformed police officer in tow. Two men and one woman knelt beside James, bringing the odor of exhaust fumes and latex with them. One of the men put down a big plastic machine with wires and electrodes.

He prepared the machine as the short-haired woman in her fifties put her blue-gloved hand on James's shoulder. "Sir, we have it from here."

James didn't stop compressions.

"Sir! You need to move aside."

The woman pushed her way into position and took over compressions. James felt his face boil. His vision went red. His only thought, like a fire alarm in his brain, was to throw her across the room and smash her into the tile wall. A thick forearm locked around James's chest and pulled him away before he could react.

"Easy, easy, easy," Brian's voice said in his ear.

James snapped his head around to see Brian's frowning face and smell the garlic on his breath. The police officer eyed James.

"I'm fine. I'm fine! Let go." James shook off Brian's hold, held his own left hand, and breathed heavily through his nose.

They cut open Derek's shirt and stuck electrodes on his body while the third paramedic hooked up a bag valve mask to a steel oxygen bottle.

"How long has he been unconscious?" the woman asked.

"I don't know... eight or nine minutes?"

"You know what he was doing?" the man working the bag-valve mask asked.

"There was another boy, a needle, and his arm. I think he overdosed on some drug—heroin, but I don't know for sure."

"Narcan," the woman said to her partner.

They slid James's glowing cell phone out of the way.

71

Suddenly James remembered the dispatcher. He grabbed his phone off the floor. "The paramedics are here. What should I do?"

"They've got it from here. Thank you for your help." She disconnected, and James stuffed the phone into his pocket.

Brian's eyes were wide, enhanced by his thick lenses.

A lightheaded fog encased James's head. "The other kid—I don't know his name—red-haired kid. I sent him to get you. He, uh... I don't know, he was in there and part of it."

Brian put a hand on James's shoulder. "You should go out in the gym. Police will probably want to talk to you. Just head out there and take a seat. You did a great job, James. We're lucky you were here to find him."

"Narcan's not working," the woman said. "Clear for shock."

The paramedics moved away from Derek's body.

"I'm clear, you're clear, we're all clear," the woman said.

"Delivering shock," the other paramedic said as he pushed a button.

Derek's pale chest shifted for a second, shaking under the power of the electricity. The paramedics eyed the still screen then jumped back into CPR.

James shook off Brian's hand and left the bathroom. He felt as if he were being lifted out of his body. His shoes were awkward and loose, the sides scraping him, the bottoms rough against his feet. The basketball court was empty. The kids must have been ushered out. James went to the nearest wall and put his back to it. His body slid down till he reached the wooden floor. Two policemen came through and propped open the doors in the court and again in the lobby. James heard the sounds of idling diesel engines outside. The two policemen walked in long, deliberate strides in James's direction. When they were close, James glanced up in time to see them push down the hall to the bathroom.

James examined his hands. He hardly recognized them as his own. They shook like dead leaves in the autumn wind. He tried to calm himself with deep breaths but found that he couldn't rid himself of the shaking. In the bathroom, the paramedics were still trying to restart Derek's heart. James put his hands on the back of his neck and slumped forward between his knees.

"James."

James rubbed his temples with his eyes closed. He thought he'd heard someone call his name. Was it in his head? He wasn't sure. It didn't matter.

"James, babe, look at me. Are you all right?"

She stood there as if summoned up by his imagination, dressed in her work attire — a gray suit and white blouse tucked into her slacks. When she bent down to get closer to him, the black handgun strapped to her waist appeared. James knew her as no one else knew her. He knew her secrets, her fragility, her tenderness, and her touch. She wasn't a hardened detective right now; she was his concerned lover.

"James, are you hurt?"

Hurt? Why would he be hurt? He remembered the blood on his sleeve. "It's not my blood, it's... Derek's."

All at once, his only desire was to get out of the gym. He leaned his shoulder blades against the wall to steady his frame and found his feet. He stared at Maya, feeling a wave of nausea.

Another paramedic, a young guy with a buzz cut and a three-inch surgery scar on his head, pushed a stretcher. Its wheels spun toward them over the gym floor. The man nodded at James then at Maya. He, too, pushed past them into the hall.

Thirty seconds later, Derek came out on the stretcher, attached to a web of wires with a plastic tube sticking out of his mouth that the bag-valve mask squeezed air through. They continued CPR as they wheeled him out of the gym and to the ambulance.

*Too much time.*

Maya embraced James as he held himself stiff and cold as a cadaver. He focused on reading the plaque on the wall behind Maya. "In loving memory of Theodore 'Teddy' Monroe, 1928-2013, who established the Monroe Recreational Center as a safe haven for the youth of Newborough."

James let go of Maya and suggested they go outside. He put his shaking hand in her firm grasp as if they were on a date, and they walked out together. The evening temperature was in the seventies, yet James was freezing. He sat on the outside steps. The ambulance had already left; he heard the sirens waning in the distance. After a minute, they faded away completely.

The police cars remained. Several passing policemen glanced at him, waiting and watching. They would want some answers, but while he was with Maya, they wouldn't approach. His hand shook within Maya's grasp. Her warmth was the only thing keeping him connected to the world of blue-and-white flashing lights, of police cruisers and yellow tape.

Eventually the sharks came for him. James retold the same events to two different detectives. When the detectives found out that James had come in contact with Derek's blood, they suggested that he go to the hospital. James refused, and they suggested he see his doctor in the next few days. They wanted him to go downtown so they could get another account for the report there, but Maya stepped in and told them that he was done for tonight. One detective who had grilled him, Wade Copley, seemed ready to protest, but she gave him a short, focused squint.

Although Maya pleaded with him to leave his moped behind, James argued that the ride would help him clear his head. His hands were no longer shaking. She agreed as long as she could follow him home.

While James drove, he listened to his engine work up a hill. His half helmet had a loose neck strap that smacked James repeatedly in the face. He barely felt the sting as it worked his cheeks over. He did, however, feel memories release from his skull like miniature geysers. In an effort to cast the images away, he shook his head as if the memories were as real as rain in his hair.

His dad's twisted face flashed. He heard Dad's voice, which even when sober was slurred and thick with anger, especially when he called his name. "James! Get your ass down here."

When James reached the bottom of the stairs, his dad was waiting. "You better change that face real quick. You got something to say to me?"

He was smart enough to keep his mouth shut.

"Going to need you all Saturday, Sunday, and Monday," his father barked.

"I've got school Monday," James said flatly.

"Nope, you're going to be roofing the house and garage with me." Dad sounded childish, his face distorted.

At that point, Mom stepped in. "Jim, he needs to go to school. Can't you do it yourself on Monday?"

The air around his dad seemed to become electrically charged. The vein in his forehead appeared like an ugly root that cracked his scalp. James often imagined crushing that vein between his thumb and index finger.

James's palms were sweating on Sally Jay's grips. His Adam's apple had been replaced with a heavy brass doorknob. He glanced in his mirror to check that Maya was still behind him.

Dad's heavy backhand caught Mom off guard that time. He picked her up off the floor and methodically slapped her face, breaking and bruising her delicate skin. James only got one punch in, a hard thud against Dad's cheek that was enough to turn his attention away from Mom.

Even drunk, Dad was much quicker and stronger than James. He grabbed James by his shirt and threw him to the kitchen floor. A knee hammered James's neck and jaw, pinning him down. The tan tiles, whose floral prints became engraved on James's face, crushed into his cheeks. The more he struggled, the more Dad forced the knee down. Dad leaned in close, the familiar odor of fish from the cannery blended with the Jameson whiskey on his breath.

He pushed down on James's rib cage, trying to crush him like a cockroach. James's ribs flexed, but one bone had had enough and split like a tree branch. James cried out, the new pain shattering his former thresholds, worse than anything he'd ever felt. The tender wound was made worse by dad's weight. Then Mom's chipped nails stabbed into Dad's shoulders. He let up long enough for James to squirm away, holding his fractured rib and praying for the pain to stop.

James slumped over Sally Jay's handlebars and tilted toward the yellow dashes striping the road. Headlights and a furious engine rushed past in the other lane. James pulled himself up and straightened out Sally Jay.

"I'm okay, I'm fine." He touched his rib. Although the cracked rib had healed on its own long ago, it was still sensitive to the touch after all these years.

James almost drove by his street. He turned onto his road and parked in front of the condo. Maya pulled in behind him.

In the dull glow of their living room, they assumed their usual positions on the couch. James found Maya's hand. Her mouth opened, but she didn't speak.

"What is it?" James asked.

She squeezed his hand tighter and rubbed her forehead. "I got a call. Derek didn't make it."

"Oh," James said, and released her hand.

"I'm so sorry." Her voice choked for a moment, and she sniffed.

"I'm going to shower now." His joints stiffened.

She wiped her eyes and rubbed his thighs. "Want me to join you?"

"No." He didn't want to sound mean, but it probably came across that way.

Hot, gushing lines combed his body. He let the water collect in his mouth. He swished it around then spit it out, hitting the knobs like a sharp shooter. If he was going to cry or vomit, he would do it here, where no one could see him. But he didn't. Derek's death seemed like something he'd seen on TV.

He turned the hot water knob a full rotation to the left, and the stream became so blistering that he felt the water burning away his dead skin as if it were a metal rake dragging across his body. Steam rose, and he lingered under the scalding water.

When he turned the water off and drew open the curtain, he stepped into a thick cloud of steam. James hadn't bothered to turn on the light when he'd come in the bathroom. He stared into the heart of the mist and swung his hand through the sheet of steam. He tried to clasp the trailing wisps, but they escaped.

He flicked on the light switch, making the fan kick on as well. He couldn't see his reflection in the fogged mirror. James lifted his fingers and drew in two eyes about where his eyes would have been. He thought of the image drawn on the dusty board game at Tucker's house. He drew a sad mouth where his mouth would have been.

On the rare occasion when he wasn't in a rush, he preferred to air dry. He left his towel on the hook and entered the bedroom naked. He heard Maya in the kitchen, humming a familiar blues tune — "Black Coffee," a song that her mother had always sung.

When they were dating, James had confessed that his father had been an alcoholic and used to hit him and his mother. His mother had seemed to wither over the years. Doctors said she'd had the cancer for years and must have known, but they found it too late for treatment. At the time, James knew it was more than her body; her will to live was fading. Just before James graduated from university, his mother left her heavy world for a lighter one. James's father seemed to age fast after her death. His binge drinking eventually killed him. Maya accepted James for his history and loved him more for it. She was a strong woman for everyone else, but with him alone, she might as well have been made of putty.

Dry but slightly chilled, James changed into sweats with a gray zip-up. He followed the scent of teriyaki sauce and grilled beef and breathed in the sweet perfume of caramelized onions sizzling amid diced potatoes. He hugged Maya from behind. She had changed into tights and a long-sleeve shirt with the sleeves pulled up. She set aside her spatula and stroked his arm.

"Aren't you still on the clock?" James asked.

Maya turned to face him and held his hand. "Sam covered for me tonight. I took his morning shift tomorrow. I can bring you in with me, and we'll get your story down so you can be done with it."

"Thanks, babe, I'm lucky to have you."

"I'm the lucky one to have a man like you, baby." She ran her hand through his damp hair and down the length of his neck. Her nails dragged down his spine.

He kissed her and mumbled into her hair that he wasn't very hungry. She made him up a plate anyway. He ate it dutifully.

When she was asleep, James stole out of bed and sat outside on the steps of his condo. He looked at the stars and once again saw Derek's lifeless body on the bathroom tile. He saw the dirty needle on the floor and the dark blood oozing out the kid's arm with each compression. The blue lips he'd tried to get Derek to breathe through again.

The steak and potatoes in his stomach felt like thick tar in a plastic grocery bag. He ran until he was in a small grove of trees and he willed his throat to heave the mess out of him. The mass in his stomach seemed to expand.

"Get out of me. Damn it. Get the hell out of me!"

His body shook, and tears fell into the moss-covered ground. He punched his stomach three times, each time harder than the last, causing a fit of dry heaves and coughs. He swung again but hit his bad rib instead. The pain went from bad to agonizing. James dropped to the ground, clutching his belly, and curled up like a grub; he concentrated on breathing. When that didn't work, he focused on the night sounds. One ear was aimed at the canopy while the other was plugged to the ground. He heard crickets rubbing their legs together. Other nameless insects tossed their rhythms into the night. The sounds grew louder, then he heard a twig snap at the edge of his grove, where the forest was dense with pines. The insects went still, as did his heart.

"Who's there?" He threw the question into the dark trees.

A shadow separated itself from a tree and retreated.

Another bout of pain erupted from James's stomach. His ear pressed to the ground felt the earth move, heard footfalls from the dark figure. The insects resumed. James stayed curled up in the grove for an hour before he went back home.

He cleaned up and eased back into bed. Maya woke when his weight shifted the bed springs. She put a hand on his cheek.

"Baby, you're cold," she said.

James shed his sweat shirt and sweatpants and pulled the covers over himself. "I'll warm up."

"Are you all right?" she asked.

James thought about the question. He slid closer to her and held her warm body against his. Maya preferred to sleep without any clothes, and James loved her for that. He had never imagined himself loving another person as much as he loved her.

James kissed her cheek lightly and whispered, "As long as I have you, I am."

# CHAPTER 10

D EREK'S DEATH HAD MADE THE front page. "Local Boy Dies of Heroin Overdose at the Monroe Recreational Center." Would parents stop sending their kids there because of this incident? James suspected some would.

Maya wanted him to go to the Critical Incident Stress Debriefing meeting. Although James was resistant, he eventually agreed. Only the people directly involved with the case were allowed to attend.

The meeting was held on Thursday, three days after Derek's death. When they arrived at the meeting, James followed Maya's lead. She'd been to these sorts of meetings before. They entered a conference room, and James smelled coffee. He realized that he had forgotten to put on deodorant, and an itchy anxiety crept over him. Being around all those cops didn't help. He spied the tiny orange light indicating hot coffee; beside the coffee sat a vegetable platter.

James was filling a small paper plate with celery and carrot sticks when a woman slid in beside him. "Mm... coffee. Nectar of the gods." She let out a childish giggle. The woman was surprisingly perky for eight in the morning.

James sipped his coffee only to have his tongue instantly retreat. "Careful, it's hot."

"I'll keep that in mind." Her voice carried the steady tone of a karate sensei.

James couldn't pin an age to her—one of those women who could be either fifty or seventy. Her face appeared young, although there were telling wrinkles around her eyes. Her body was stringy, her skin resembling the underside of a leaf, yet her overall appearance was that of a sturdy woman.

"I didn't see you at the incident. Are you a nurse or doctor?" James asked, waiting for her to fill in the blank. It was awkward referring to Derek's death as "the incident."

"I'm a doctor of sorts—a psychiatrist—but no, I wasn't on scene. I'm Carol." She offered her hand, and her eyes achieved a steady focus on James's face. "I lead these Critical Incident Stress Debriefings. What a mouthful that is to say, huh?"

"James Morrow." He shook her hand. Her sudden interest in him gave James the sense of being prepped for dissection. Had someone told her that he was the guy who'd found Derek? The sorry social worker who'd never held a boy's life in his hands? He wondered if she had latched on to him purposely. "If you'll excuse me, I'm going to take my seat. Place is starting to fill up."

Carol smiled and sipped her coffee. Her light-handed application of lipstick left a subtle red imprint on her cup.

He wandered back toward his seat, nodding and giving little quick smiles to the men and women milling about the room. He recognized the paramedics clustered together in one part of the room and saw police officers mingling back and forth between the firefighters and detectives. James's chair had been usurped by Sam. Maya's back was to James as she leaned in to speak with Sam.

"All right, everyone, please have a seat. We're going to start." Carol had taken a place at the head of the three linked foldable plastic tables. She stood and wrote her name on a whiteboard balanced on an easel.

James found a seat next to Detective Wade Copley.

Wade bounced a piece of gum in his mouth and faced James. "James Morrow. First it was the bridge fisherman suicide and now a kid overdosing at the rec center." Wade chuckled. "At the station, we have a name for guys like you."

"Oh, yeah, what's that?" James chewed a carrot as he gazed at Wade's dull expression.

"Black cloud. Whenever you're around, bad things tend to happen."

"Sounds a bit superstitious to me."

"Yeah, well, time will tell, right?"

Carol spread her hands wide. "I want to thank you all for coming to this Critical Incident Stress Debriefing. For those of you who don't know me, my name is Carol Wayneright, and I'm a licensed psychiatrist. I help the state conduct these debriefings. I also run a private office right here in Newborough." Carol paused for a moment. "We came here today because there was a traumatic event in our community for emergency workers and normal, everyday folks alike."

James didn't see Brian anywhere. He was probably dealing with the legal issues. Maya had explained that activity at the center had been suspended until the police finished their investigation. James already missed the kids.

"At this point, I would like to let you know that I have been given the information about the incident. I want you to be aware that we are all bound by law to keep whatever is said here private." Her eyes moved to several of the men and women in her audience. "My goal today is to go over some important strategies to manage stress."

Carol talked about how an untimely death could cause more of an emotional strain than an elderly person who had lived a long life. She talked about the body's responses, including sleep problems, depression, anger, and addiction.

"Does anyone have any ideas on what are the top causes of stress?" she asked.

James perked up.

"Divorce," a firefighter said, earning some light laughter from the room.

"Yes, divorce is definitely top five," Carol said.

"Medical bills," the paramedic next to James offered.

The other paramedic nodded knowingly.

"Yes, anything medical-related: injuries, diseases, or overwhelming hospital bills. Definitely up there. What else?"

"Public speaking." That came from Gary McCourt, the police chief.

The whole room murmured their approval.

Carol gave a fake wipe of her brow. "You bet, Chief. I'm sweating bullets right now."

That prompted another round of chuckles from table.

"Death of a loved one," Maya's soft voice said. Her eyes met James for a moment then dropped back to her folded hands.

Carol nodded. "Are there any couples in the room, by chance?"

The detectives and cops turned their attention toward Maya and James. James raised his hand dutifully, and Maya followed.

"That's great. Yes, Maya, you got the number one cause of stress: losing a spouse."

Sweat hung from his armpit hair like dripping stalactites. What a day to forget deodorant.

"This leads into how stress can interfere with relationships." Carol led into the next portion, and James felt the eyes leave him.

The ball of his right foot worked the floor, and he wiped his palms on his tan pants while his knee bounced. He sipped his coffee then pushed the cup away. Caffeine wouldn't help calm his nerves.

"And this can lead to a lack of sex drive," Carol said, finishing a statement James hadn't heard.

James wanted to glance at Maya but was too afraid she would be looking back at him. He locked his eyes on Carol and listened.

"My last goal is to talk about managing the emotions that you now know how to recognize. Here are my suggestions." She gave a Mr. Universe pose. "Go out and exercise. When you work out or do something active, your body releases endorphins, which we all know makes us feel better. Smile, because even if you don't feel happy, the act of smiling releases endorphins." Carol showed everyone in the room what a smile looked like, which was silly, but James counted more than one cop in the room who might actually benefit from her demonstration. "Have a beer. I know all the medical people in the room probably know that alcohol is a depressant, but one or two beers can actually be good for relieving stress. Of course, as with many things, if done in excess, drinking will have negative effects."

She concluded the meeting and set a stack of her business cards at the end of the table. James circled around to meet Maya. He thanked Carol and swiped one of her cards, nonchalantly slipping it into the safety of his pocket.

# CHAPTER 11

T HE PADDLE'S BLADE SLICED THROUGH the water, leaving behind miniature whirlpools spiraling in James's wake. The sea kayak was more streamlined and narrow than the river kayaks he was used to. The long craft seemed to glide over the water as if he were ice-skating. The kayak rental shop, which was a stone's skip away from Denny's Clam Shack, put him right back on Crooked Creek. It'd been a seed of a thought that grew into a plan; with Maya at work and him with the Saturday off, why not try kayaking?

James waved at two fishermen, a father and his boy, standing at the edge of one of the passing docks. The father's rod suddenly bowed like thistle in the wind. Once he had the fish hooked, he thrust the rod into his son's chubby hands. The boy reeled the line in wildly, his tongue shoved out and to the corner of his lips. The father cheered his son on and helped him lift the mackerel, shaking for dear life, out of the water. The fish hit the dock and flapped its shining body, catching swatches of sun on the scales of its silver underbelly. The boy giggled and tried to grab the slippery fish.

James pushed his shades back up to the bridge of his nose and put his paddle blades back to work. He stopped when he got to a section of the creek that opened wide. He heard the whir of an engine and voices clearly, as if they were only a few feet away. That was a trick that the water played. He peered over his shoulder.

"Go faster, go faster… he landed it!"

The voices were coming from a speed boat. The teenager at

the wheel was a skinny kid with a helmet of brown hair and no shirt. Another kid, who looked much the same, was giving the driver the play-by-play of their buddy, who was at the end of a tow rope. The wake boarder was carving the water, shooting through the air across the boat's wake. The driver's eyes met James's, and the kid smiled.

James recognized mischief in that look and decided he was too close to the middle of the creek for his liking. With quick wind-milling strokes, he paddled toward the shore. The boy veered the boat until he was nearly on top of James then turned sharply away.

The wide grin and wild eyes of the wake boarder locked in the image of a lunatic as he used the centrifugal force to launch over the boat's wake as it reached James's kayak. James watched the front of the boy's board reach James's eye level at its peak. The boy had miscalculated his jump. James saw the flash of horror in the kid's face.

James twisted his body away, and the kayak came with him. A fistful of brackish water punched down his throat. Upside down and under the water, he felt the tangle of the paddle and the awkwardness of his life jacket. He pushed the paddle away from him. He was encased in cloudy water and a furious stream of his own bubbles. He heard the hurried thrum of the sport boat's propeller blades slicing the water; the sound rapidly faded away.

James wriggled to escape. His foot was jammed. He would have to roll himself back to the surface. His lungs yearned for air. Frantic images and half-thoughts burst into his head. He attempted to flip back over. The kayak rocked but not enough. Another try—no good. The plastic cut into his leg. Steely silverfish crawled into his blurry vision. James rocked some more, starting to feel lightheaded.

That was when he saw Derek Fanning, his pale face submerged under the green water, his long hair floating, wearing the same Metallica shirt and ripped jeans. Derek swam toward James. His voice whispered in James's head, "Why did you let me die, Mr. Jay?" His lifeless eyes fixed on James, and his pale fingers reached for him. "It was my first time. I didn't want to die. Don't go. Stay down here with me."

Adrenaline pounded through his body. James raked his arms through the water, clawing for the surface. His vision turned red. He screamed through clenched teeth. *Maya!*He gathered the last of his strength and leaned hard and sharp with all of his weight, using his hands to push against the water. The kayak rolled with him this time. His mouth momentarily breached. He forced air into his lungs before he was dunked back under. Derek was there, under the water and waiting. He grabbed James's arm, holding him under. James struggled and batted the hand away. He heaved again and captured another breath of air. Then he felt the kayak release his lower half. He surfaced and breathed raggedly, coughing up brackish water.

With the inside of his nose stinging and his strength drained, he let the life vest do its job and support his weight. After he caught his breath, he paddled weakly over to the flipped kayak, grabbed the grip at the front, and dragged it along as he kicked toward shore. He found the paddle floating close by, and when his feet touched dry land, he shed his gear and sprawled out on the sand bar. For a while he lay there, eyes closed, grateful to suck in air and content to let the sun burn his forehead. Derek had seemed so real. Was it some sort of oxygen-deprived hallucination? He wiped water out of his eyes and realized he'd lost his sunglasses to the muddy river bottom.

"Ahoy there."

James recognized the voice and craned his neck, his hand shading his eyes. Tucker shouted from the deck of the *Periwinkle* as he came toward James's small patch of shore.

A short time later, he and his kayak were aboard the *Periwinkle*, and James recounted his brush with death.

"Shit, man," Tucker said. "Damn kids."

"Just stupid—"

"Hey," Tucker injected, "you hear about that kid at the rec center the other day?"

The center and the bathroom, would those places ever feel normal again? Or would they haunt him? "I did."

Tucker rubbed sweat from his sideburns. "He overdosed, I heard. You know the boy?"

James flipped a five-gallon bucket upside down and used it for a seat. "I knew him." He watched the steady froth of the boat wake and listened to the murmur of the engine as the boat cruised up the creek.

"It's a damn shame." Tucker's tone carried a genuine sadness.

"It is," James said to his hands. He turned his attention to Tucker. "I heard from my buddy Bill that you were working for him now."

Tucker nodded and winked at James over his shoulder. "That's right. Working every night doing security. It's nice to have a steady paycheck coming in again."

"And Kathy got ahold of you?"

"Yeah, we're making payments on the house again. Going to be a long road, but I think we'll live long enough to give the bank their money back."

"How's Kevin doing?" James asked.

"Good. He wasn't happy to see the rec center closed down, but he's going to try out for the school basketball team once school starts back up in the fall."

James tilted his head. "It's only temporary. They're closed until the police finish their investigation."

Tucker left one hand on the wheel and faced James. "You didn't hear?"

"What?" James wiped sweat off his forehead.

Tucker sighed and rubbed his scruffy cheek. "The mother of the kid who died is suing. They're going to close down indefinitely."

"Shit." James had been so caught up in his own bullshit that he hadn't realized the center was in so much trouble. *Goddamn sue-happy sons of bitches! At least wait for your son to be buried before you start grabbing for money from a fucking non-profit.* His teeth grinded, and he massaged his jaw.

Tucker guided the *Periwinkle* around a green marker buoy.

He spoke over his shoulder. "Hey, I don't know what your plans are, but I'm going to hit up the bar after I dock. You should come along."

James heard himself agree.

---

While he folded laundry in the bedroom, a curled up bit of paper detached itself from his half-folded towel—Carol Wayneright's business card from two days ago.

"I'm home," Maya called from downstairs.

James shoved the card into his wallet and went back to the laundry. He grabbed her black thong from the pile of unfolded clothes, stretched the material, and fired the underwear at her as she stepped into the room. She laughed as she defended herself from the flying lace.

Maya dropped her cuffs, service gun, one of her two 9mm backup guns, and her badge into the gun safe. She put her jacket on a hanger and walked over to kiss James. After they moved apart, she puckered her lips. "Have you been drinking?"

"I had a beer." A frown dented Maya's face, so James said, "I went kayaking today and met up with Tucker. We stopped by a bar afterward and had a drink."

"I've never seen you drink before. I thought you were against it?"

"I'm not *against* drinking. I'm *against* abusing alcohol. Besides, the psychiatrist said a beer would help release stress."

The hand she put on her hip partnered up with the slitted stare she gave him. "Yeah, I heard her." Maya matched a pair of James's socks and rolled them in a ball. "Is everything okay, babe?"

"Everything's fine. Why?"

"You've had a lot of stress lately, and I've been consumed with work. Just want to check in on my man."

"I'm good—"

"Oh, look! It's like a little baby sock." Maya held up her shrunken white cotton sock, offering it to James.

89

He grabbed the sock and toyed with the stitching, then sifted through the pile until he found the mate. "Babe, you still want to have a baby with me, right?"

"Of course." Maya smashed her lips into his mouth. She grabbed his lower lip with her teeth. "More than anything."

Her love had always been so unconditional. At first he'd been wary of her commitment to him and their future. They'd fought but never over anything big enough to cause their relationship to falter. He stared into her brown eyes. He would do anything to keep her happy. "Good, then strip." He brushed the remaining laundry off the bed.

"Ah-ha. I like this side of you." Maya gave him a sideways grin as she yanked off her shirt and shimmied out of her pants.

James dimmed the lights while she revealed the familiar curves that stirred him to life.

# CHAPTER 12

"I THOUGHT I MIGHT SEE YOU again."

James nodded to Dr. Wayneright. The chair he'd chosen was a big, brown, leathery brute. It felt new, and the cushion he sat on sank deep under his weight. James tried to mold his body to the leather. The chair's arms made him feel as if he were sitting in an oversized tea cup. It was hard not to feel small, as if he were a child in his father's work boots. Pins and needles stabbed at his fingertips. He let go of the chair's arms and laced his fingers together over his kneecap.

"I beg your pardon?" James asked.

"It's good to see you again."

"It's good to see you too, Dr. Wayneright."

"Please, call me Carol."

*What am I doing here? How did I get here?* The silence tucked in around him; he sank deeper into his chair, which practically pulled him down to the carpet. She appeared to be waiting for something. Hadn't he done his part in calling and scheduling a meeting? Wasn't it *her* job to get this thing started?

"What brought—"

"Tell me—"

Their words collided.

"Ladies first," James said.

Carol smiled. "What I was going to ask was what brought you here today?"

"I needed someone to talk to... not my wife and not a friend."

"I'm honored you chose me. What's on your mind?"

James had tried to prepare his words. He'd phrased the

91

questions so well in his apartment and said them out loud to himself on the ride over, but somehow the words had leaked out of his head. "To be honest, I'm not sure." Maybe he was wrong in coming here. "I guess I just need someone to talk to."

"All right, let's talk." She switched to crossing her other leg and held her chin with her left hand.

They talked about work and Maya and exchanged tidbits of their lives. The conversation remained light until Carol said, "I've noticed you haven't mentioned anything about your own family or your childhood. I'd love to hear about how you grew up."

This was where he would have to step carefully. Glass was all around his bare feet now. "I was raised in Newborough. My family was lower-middle class." He paused.

Carol gave him a look that said to go on.

"I was an only child, as good a kid as any really. Not spoiled or needy or anything like that. I avoided trouble for the most part."

"Tell me about your parents."

"My mother passed away from cancer, and my dad died of liver failure."

"What were they like when you were younger?" she asked.

"My mother was a kind woman; she would help out anyone if she could. My father and mother were both from Massachusetts. They met on vacation—a sports bar in Florida. They fell for each other, got married, and had me."

"Your mom sounds like a gentle woman. What was your dad like?"

"Strict, but then again, his father was a mean son of bitch, so I count myself lucky." James was certain she was waiting for him to get to the point. She wasn't an idiot, and James wasn't fooling anyone. He'd taken her card, called her office, set up an appointment during his lunch break, and agreed to pay the fee. *I might as well tell her.* "From time to time, he would give me and my mother a beating when he was drunk or pissed off."

Carol's eyebrows knit together, and her lips remained

flat. "You think that might have something to do with why you're here?"

*Of course that's why I'm here.* "Might have something to do with it."

"How did you feel when your dad was hitting you and your mother?"

James sighed. What he wanted to say was that he'd felt pathetic, useless, as if he'd done something wrong. Or how he'd felt worthless and, most of all, angry. "I didn't care much about myself, but I hated when he hit my mom. She was a small woman, barely over five feet and not even a hundred pounds, and he was a pretty strong guy."

"Go on."

"I felt mad and angry. I'd just see red, you know? Problem was that I was too small to fight him off. When I tried, he put me in my place real quick. They got to know me pretty well at the hospital." James was amazed at how easy the words were flowing.

"What did you tell them at the hospital?"

"*He* told me to lie. So I did. I told them I was practicing to be a wrestler, like Hulk Hogan."

Carol nodded, and a glimmer of a smile revealed itself. The legal notepad on her lap fell forward at an angle, and James could make out neat, cursive ink marks on the page. What did those notes say?

She must have noticed him peeping at her notepad, because she shifted the pad to a higher angle. "James, an abusive parent has the potential to deeply scar a child. It's completely normal to want to leave those memories buried. I, on the other hand, have always been a firm believer that we are the products of our memories, for better or worse. They make us into the people we are. Owning and understanding the traumatic times in our lives is very important. There is no way we can realize this as children, but we can deal with our memories as adults. Every day people come to me, seeking closure or to understand times of anger and confusion. I work with them, sometimes prescribing medications, but not without first trying to work through the emotions. Any doctor can push drugs, but real healing comes from dealing with our memories with a sober mind. I like to think that we're actors in a play. The important scenes help to build our characters. Trauma is drama, and violence and tragedy tests the will of any hero." As Carol spoke, she used her hands like a true orator. Her voice was strong, yet very calm. "It's very important not to downplay incidents and moments in our lives that impact our psyche."

"I *want* to own my memories. But *his* genes are in me. What if I become just like him?"

"Even if we are simply products of our genetics, don't you also have your mother's genes in you? The gentle woman you described sounds like she had a hand in creating the humble man I see before me today."

He rubbed the back of his neck.

"The question I have for you is: are you willing to relive some of the bad memories and share them with me? To better understand what really was happening?"

James had taken the first step through the glass. He was nervous and hesitant, but beneath that was determination. "Where do we start?"

# CHAPTER 13

"GO AHEAD AND BRING US in," Tucker said.
James followed the order and pulled the *Periwinkle* by the bowline and walked the boat into the sun-warmed shallows of the faint strip of beach.

"That's close enough," Tucker said.

Maya, Melanie, and Kevin followed cue, stepping out of the *Periwinkle* and lunging through the water until their toes touched dry sand.

Tucker dropped anchor, nodding toward Maya and Melanie. "Seems like our ladies are settling in fine."

The wives had already stripped down to their bathing suits: Maya in a dark-blue bikini and sunglasses and Melanie in a red one-piece with a nearly transparent skirt wrapped around her waist, and a wide-brimmed straw hat. They were laying out their blankets, chatting as if they'd known each other their entire lives.

"Women," Tucker said.

"Yup," James acknowledged.

It was the fourth of July, and they'd spent the first half of the day cruising the Isles of Shoals. Tucker schooled them on the islands making up the cluster just ten miles off the New Hampshire coast. They'd left the boat anchored to investigate the island called Smuttynose, which was nothing more than a weathered pile of rocks and patchy vegetation protruding out of the ocean.

The sole human inhabitant, the island's steward, came out

of his brown-and-red cabin to greet them with, "You're in luck — you've picked the worst time to come to the island."

They soon discovered the truth of his remark as they followed the trail around the island. Smuttynose's other residents, vast numbers of nesting seagulls, had picked that week to have their eggs hatch. Little gray puffball chicks balancing on chopstick legs stayed close to their ground nests, crying as their infuriated parents dive-bombed the *Periwinkle's* little party of adventurers.

The steward, a short man with a graying beard and spectacles, explained the small island's history, a past punctuated by murder. The infamous Smuttynose Murders had occurred in March of 1873. Most New Englanders had probably heard the story at one time or another. A desperate man, Louis Wagner, had rowed a dory from the mainland at night to rob the island inhabitants. Instead, he stumbled upon some of the fishermen's women asleep. From what the steward could remember, Wagner had been convicted of brutally killing two of the women with an axe. The lone survivor, Maren Hontvet, had escaped the house and hid in a cave at the other end of the island. Louis Wagner was eventually sentenced and hanged for the violent murders, earning the legend and the moniker: the Smuttynose Murderer.

After the Isles of Shoals, they trolled for stripers and blue fish, coming up with empty lures. Hot and eager to swim, they made their way back to the Newborough Harbor and pulled into the beach at Smith's Cove, which served as a small state park and a sanctuary for boaters. During World War II, the bluff above the cove had housed artillery. Now only concrete bunkers remained.

James laid out his towel beside Maya then ran back into the water. He dove in headlong and let the water envelop his body. Through blurry vision, he searched the sandy bottom, expecting to see Derek's face. He swam farther out and plunged under the water again. As James kicked, something grabbed hold of his leg. James bucked violently. The thing held on for a moment then let go. James swam as hard as he could toward Tucker's boat then glanced back to see a masked face bob to the surface. Kevin removed his snorkel and coughed up seawater in his fit of laughter.

"Kevin, you maniac! You scared the crap out of me!" James stood up, the water only reaching his chest.

Kevin swam closer. "Maniac? Who says that? Weirdo." Kevin splashed James.

"Hey! Cut that out! Oh, now you're in for it."

They got in a splashing fight until Kevin swallowed a mouthful of water, which called for a time out. Kevin said he was done but not before he went under the water and kicked a fountain on James.

James watched Kevin swim back toward the beach. Farther up, he saw Maya and Melanie still talking beside the sleeping form of Tucker. James let himself float about the shallow cove. Water ran into his ears. He tuned in to the underwater sounds: a distant motor dicing up the channel, the heavy splashes of big rocks being lobbed into the water by kids off the jetty. The predominant noise was the rhythm of his breathing. He breathed in, then out, then in, and then held.

James heard his father's words. "That's right, James. Look down the sight then breathe. In, then out, then in, then hold... now shoot!"

James had been spooked by his father's urgency just as he'd pulled the trigger, making him shoot high above the beer can target.

He saw his father slap his own hip and turn away then snap back and say, "Damn it, haven't you been listening to a thing I've told you? Clean the fucking wax out of your ears and pay attention. Hold your breath. Your body needs to be still as a fucking tree. Then you need to slowly squeeze the trigger. You're pulling like, like, I don't know, your damn finger's on fire." His father's voice trailed off as he let the green bottle of Jameson perch on his lips. Then he leaned back, and the dark fluid poured into him. "This time, do better. You hear me? Shoot the fucking can. We're not leaving till you do."

James nodded, the revolver heavy in his twelve-year-old

hands. The handgun's kick worried him but not as much as his father's wrath.

He spied the can propped up on a tree stump twenty yards away. Dad had brought him shooting as a reward for doing a good day's work with no "fuck ups." The sand pits were a crummy reward, and the fact that he was alone with his father, liquor, and a gun made James so nervous that pulling the trigger seemed almost less stressful. This time he would hit the can. If he did, his father would smile and he could go home.

James pulled back the hammer and held the gun the way his father had shown him. Breathe in, breathe out, breathe in... he took aim, praying that the bullet would follow his sight. He caught his breath.

"Shoot!" his father yelled.

James closed his eyes and felt the bullet leave the barrel. When he opened his eyes, the beer can had vanished.

"Good shot. Guess you're not retarded after all." High praise. "Now hand over the gun."

James stared at the gun in his hand. The metal was still warm from the shot. A hint of sweat glistened between his palm and the rough handle. He saw the gun in his hands then saw his father. If he could hit the can at twenty yards...

"You hear me?"

James shuddered and handed the gun back to his father, who yanked it out of his grip. He capped the whiskey bottle, and they loaded themselves into the truck. As the truck bounced on the washed-out road, James glanced back, thinking how, like the can, he could have made his father disappear too.

As he floated in the cove, James shivered. A cold spot must have found him. He reflected on the memory that had floated to the surface. They were occurring more and more frequently. Sometimes they came in fragments; other times they were like home movies. Carol claimed that it was good for him to think about the confusing moments of his childhood. His memory couldn't hurt him. He understood that his anger as a boy had stiffened to the resentment he harbored toward his deceased father. Still, he wanted to understand the man, understand his violent nature and figure out what made his father hurt his own family.

During his last session, James had told Carol about seeing Derek when he'd almost drowned kayaking. She'd said that as long as he understood what was real and what was in his head, the hallucinations couldn't hurt him. Carol believed that it wasn't abnormal to hallucinate about someone shortly after their death, especially because of the circumstances and James's mental status at the time.

James waded back up the beach and let the sun heat his back.

He had told Maya about his lunch-hour Tuesday therapy sessions with Carol. Maya had praised him for finally stepping up; however, it annoyed her that he had kept it from her.

But she'd forgiven him and said, "I'm proud of you, Jamesey. Hopefully this will help you with your anger."

James hadn't had any sort of breakdowns since meeting with Carol, which he counted as a personal victory.

James walked over to where Kevin was building a sand castle. "You know the tide will take it away if you build that close," James warned.

Kevin ignored him.

Tucker and Maya were in the middle of a conversation when James fell onto his towel.

"That was wicked sweet," Tucker said. He pointed at Maya. "I've never seen a woman toss a guy like that. You dropped him on his ass!" Tucker spoke with a child-like excitement James hadn't heard from him before.

Maya scrunched up her face. "Ah, you saw that?"

Maya's department had made a big drug bust three weeks earlier. Three hundred fifty pounds of marijuana were seized along with six bags of ecstasy. The total value of the seizure: more than a quarter million dollars.

Maya continued, "That wasn't the stash we were searching for, but it's good to get those drugs off the street." She put a hand on James's shoulder.

James napped, waking up a short time later to scratch drool from his dry lips. The sun was trying to finish its daily commute to the western horizon. He put his elbow in the sand and held his head up to watch Maya. She was helping Kevin defend his castle from the rising tide. Maya laughed as she and Kevin used their hands to dig a moat, diverting the water away from the main structure. The sand was already soft and on the verge of sliding into the approaching waves.

Kevin must have realized the futility of it all, because he kicked away the castle spire. Maya laughed and joined in the destruction. Together they stomped it into a lumpy hill and ran into the water to wash the sand off of their bodies. James rarely got to see her this way, so carefree and goofy. She caught him watching her and gave him a mock serious face.

The beach had mostly cleared out, and Melanie shook sand off the towels. Tucker was already aboard the *Periwinkle*. James stood and shook out his own towel. His rough shorts scraped against his chafing legs. Maya came over to him. She grabbed his hand, and they kissed. Her lips were warm.

They stood next to each other, staring at the blue water, so close that James could smell the coconut and pineapple oils lathered on her ebony skin.

Maya put her hand on James's chest. "I need to tell you something."

James laughed. "What is it, babe?"

"Okay, all right. I'm just going to say it. " Maya threw her hands up framing her smiling face. "I'm pregnant."

James felt his eyes and mouth open wide. He put his hands on his hips. "Wow."

Maya's eyes searched his face.

James rubbed his chin. "You're pregnant? Really? Are you sure?"

"I peed on three different sticks. All the tests say 'yes.'"

James blew out a long exhale. "This is amazing! I'm going to be a dad."

"The best dad!" She grabbed his shoulders and kissed him hard.

"I'm going to be a dad," James said louder then laughed. He hugged Maya and the life within her. "We're going to be parents." James wiped tears from the corner of his eyes and kissed her over and over.

# CHAPTER 14

T HE BREAK ROOM WINDOW GAVE James a chance to observe the leftover rain from the storm. It was a true nor'easter, which meteorologists had predicted would be taken out to sea. Instead, the storm pounded up the eastern seaboard with a vengeance, a real mid-summer swashbuckler that rallied off the Cape and forced itself upon the coastal parts of New Hampshire and Maine.

James sipped his coffee as news reporters spit information at him.

"Hundreds of trees have fallen, leaving thousands of Granite Staters without power and many homes and vehicles destroyed."

Maya had been working overtime since the start of the storm. She'd abandoned her regular duties to respond to emergency calls.

"The Newborough weather station reports over eight inches of rain with gusts of above seventy-five miles per hour. The surplus rain has put many rivers over their banks, causing flooding and road closures across the eastern side of the state."

James was lucky that their condo complex had been built on high ground; they didn't have to worry about dragging out a sump pump for a flooded basement.

"This video, shot July fifteenth, at the height of the storm, is from a local Rye man."

Angry waves poured over the concrete seawalls and flooded streets and parking lots. What about Tucker? No way he would have gone out in such a storm, but what about his traps?

The anchorman, with parted brown hair and a baby face,

turned to his fellow anchorwoman, a blond whose red lipstick matched her red suit jacket. With a tacked-on sense of empathy, he said, "Truly a record-breaking summer storm that has battered the seacoast, leaving many residents shaken up but ready to pick up the pieces."

After work, James called Tucker's house. "Melanie? Hi, it's James."

"What do you need?" She sounded rushed.

"Nothing, I just wanted to see if Tucker's traps were all right—the storm and all."

"It's not good," Melanie said.

"Do you think Tucker needs some help?"

"I don't know. Ask him yourself!"

"Mom, I need you," Kevin said in the background.

"One second, Kev." Melanie sighed. "Listen, Tucker left early this morning. Try calling back tomorrow. I'm sorry, but things are a little hectic around here."

James apologized, but she had already hung up.

The next day, the sun came out and revealed land ravished by the summer storm. Trash littered the streets. Orange-vested public works crews picked up debris and cleared the roads. Scattered traffic cones lay fallen in puddles, waiting to be retrieved. The old colonials dripped rain water from leaks in their gutters. Cars splashed through pools.

He waited until noon to call the Flynns. After two rings, Kevin picked up the phone.

"Hey, Kevin, it's James Morrow. Is your dad around?"

"He said he would be gone all day again—at the beach."

"Are his traps all right?" James asked.

"I don't know and don't care."

"At the beach, you said? Which beach?"

"Probably all of them," Kevin said.

"Kevin, is everything all right at home? Are you and your mom okay?"

James heard a female voice say something in the background, too muffled to understand.

"I have to go," Kevin said.

"Hold on one second—"

"I have to go, bye," Kevin said before the phone disconnected.

James swerved Sally Jay around the flooded potholes as he cleared the downtown area and headed toward the coast. At the first beach he passed, a state beach, he had his first view of the waves. Large rolling dumpers splashed white water over the dark-blue, glassy ocean surface. The waves fell then gathered their strength and reformed until they sped over the dark-brown stretches of sand. A dozen surfboards bobbed joyously among the eastern giants. Black wetsuits made the surfers resemble seals instead of people.

On the beach, head-high piles of debris, mostly filled with lobster traps, were stacked like unlit bonfires. James squinted, searching the colored buoys twisted among the crushed black, green, and yellow traps.

Coming up to the next beach, he spied Tucker's truck sitting alone in the parking lot. James parked and walked to the top of the small rise of sand overlooking the beach. Standing amid the knee-high beach grass and clumps of crushed weeds, James scanned the beach. The waves were much tamer here; no surfers bothered with them. Seagulls strutted like wind-up toys, leaving trails of webbed footprints that were washed away with each passing wave. The birds stopped only to crane their necks and cry out at the sky. James couldn't overlook the mountain of traps that had been dragged out of the sea and left in the dry, gray sand just beyond the high tide mark.

Then there was Tucker, sitting alone in the damp sand, a stone's throw from the waves, staring at the ocean.

James's black leather shoes sank three quarters of an inch into the soft, shifting sand with each step; his pant legs pulled tight at the knees. His tie, blown by the wind, flopped like a fish out of water. He brushed his hand to settle his tie as a rush of air tossed sand against his shirt and through his black hair, which was growing shaggy and steadily trying to invade his ears. As James passed the tangle of metal cages, he couldn't look away from the painted buoys amid the tangle of ruined traps. Most were blue and white, Tucker's colors.

Tucker's powerful shoulders were sunken forward.

James cleared his throat and swung around wide to see his face. "Hey" was all he could think to say.

After a moment, Tucker blinked several times, seeming to wake up from a dream. "James?" His voice sounded ragged. He coughed a short harsh hack, licked his lips, then asked, "The hell you doing here?"

"I could ask the same of you."

Tucker lifted a buoy that had been partially concealed by his bent legs. He stuck the post in the soft sand and spun the buoy like a spindle from a bow drill. James half expected smoke to curl out of the hole the post was making in the sand.

Tucker breathed out a sigh, and James thought he heard him say something, some small flex of vocal chords that sounded like "cursed."

"I called—"

Tucker cut him off. "Gone—just one storm—poof." Tucker grabbed a chunk of damp sand and tried to make it fly away like white dust from a magic act. The sand proved too moist and stuck to his fingers. He flung it away in disgust. "I ain't never seen a storm trash this many traps—never." As he spoke, he seemed to be talking to the sea.

James felt uncomfortable standing so high above him. He kicked away a patch of kelp and settled down next to him in the wet sand. There was no pretty way to do it.

Tucker seemed unwilling to obey the rhythm of a normal conversation, and he remained quiet for a while. James didn't face him; instead, he stared at the ocean. As he gazed out across the blue majesty, all James could think about was how the wet sand had soaked through to his boxers.

"How many traps do you have left?" James asked.

"Fifty, if I'm lucky."

"Oh," James said. He'd helped Tucker pull up more than fifty traps, and a bucketload of keepers wouldn't be much against high gas prices. He'd mentioned that he had nine hundred traps. That had to be tens of thousands of dollars in gear. "Insurance?"

Tuckers wiped his lips. "Nope."

"If there's any way I can help you out—"

"Stop! I'm through taking charity." He let the buoy drop. It rolled in an arc toward the ocean then fishtailed to a halt. "I'll think of something. I'll figure a way out of this mess." A change came over Tucker's eyes, his concentration interrupted by the shade of a passing cloud that slid over the sun like a pulled curtain. "You know, me and you aren't so different."

"How's that?"

"My dad beat me too." Tucker eyed James.

James remembered how he'd let that information slip the day he went lobstering with Tucker. "I'm sorry to hear that. We're the cracks in the system, I guess."

Tucker shook his head. "No, we're more like lobsters. Bottom-feeders, plucked out of the ocean to feed the rich."

James nodded. "Can I at least help with hauling these traps off the beach?"

"Thanks, but no thanks. These are mine and my father's traps. It's only right that I'm the one to put them to rest." Tucker left the buoy lying abandoned on the sand.

Tucker stood first, then James found his feet and casually glanced at his watch. Three o'clock—he'd gone over his lunch hour. James looked up to see Tucker studying him.

"You better get back to work," Tucker said.

*I'm sorry. I'll be here if you need me. What can I do to help? I'll be around...* James couldn't string together the proper words, so he settled with, "Give me a call if you need—I mean, *want* to talk."

Tucker nodded and turned away to face the ocean, as if dismissing him.

As James passed the heap of traps for the second time, the bent and twisted cages seemed to remind him of the bars of a prison cell.

# CHAPTER 15

MAYA RECLINED IN HER STIFF office chair and spun around the only thought on her mind: where was the heroin coming from? Recent leads had turned into nothing but dead ends. She suspected that the drugs had gone underground in response to recent media attention. Her mind turned to the boy who had helped Derek Fanning overdose at the rec center. The redheaded juvenile had turned out to be the only son of a wealthy local businessman: Fred Hanson, the type of man who rubbed elbows with the town councilmen. Hanson had delivered his son to the station to turn himself in but not without a lawyer strapped to his side.

The boy's trial would be drawn out; he would more than likely to settle for a plea bargain. Lady Justice seemed to lift up her blindfold and wink at the privileged.

Maya sipped a bottle of orange juice and rubbed her eyelids. After working overtime from last week's storm, she'd surrendered the rest of her free time to preparing for the baby. She and James had seen their baby during the ultrasound yesterday. Maya cried when the doctor detected the heartbeat, and even James had misty eyes when the screen showed their blip of a baby, which at six weeks from her last period, was the size of a watermelon seed.

"Chief wants you switched over to light duty starting tomorrow, Maya."

The voice behind her severed her thoughts. Maya put a hand to her chest and turned away from her computer screen. "Wade, jeez, I just lost two years of my life."

"You're too edgy," he said.

"You're too hairy," Maya countered.

Wade looked down at the tuft of chest hair that sprang forth from the unbuttoned top button of his shirt. Wade had been a detective on the Newborough Police Department longer than anyone else.

"Light duty? We'll see about that." Maya chuckled then turned, giving him a view of her back.

"Chief's orders," Wade said. "So what did we end up getting out of that kid?"

Maya glanced up from her keyboard. He was leaning over her and close enough that she could smell his strong aftershave. She wrinkled her nose. No small wonder why his ex-wife had moved to California.

"What kid?" she asked.

"The freaking kid! Hanson's son—the OD case at the rec. Wasn't that long ago, so don't play me for a retard."

"Jesus," Maya said in a hushed tone. She rolled her eyes, and her fingers busied themselves typing up an overdue narrative.

"What? Mad Dog Maya can't handle talking shop with the boys?" He sat on the corner of her desk, picked up a small stack of paper, and thumbed through the pages.

The guys in the department had given her a heavy dose of credit for the way she'd body-slammed Ricky Vasquez. Wade had even recorded the news footage and gone as far as to set up a TV in the station. Every badge in the department had stopped to watch her toss Ricky to the ground. They had replayed the footage dozens of times, hooting like excited chimps each time Ricky was dropped. She would be lying to herself if she said it hadn't given her some satisfaction. As a result, the nickname "Mad Dog Maya" had been floating around the coffeepots, and apparently it had stuck.

"You know, a killer like you ought to be able to answer a simple question."

Maya stopped typing. She gave in and turned on him. Wade's face was hidden behind the papers he was pretending to read.

"What did you call me?"

"A killer." Wade dropped the packet on the desk. "You're a sharpshooter—the Vasquez raid. Is memory loss a pregnancy thing?"

If he was trying to soften his comments, he was doing a miserable job. She looked into his face then at his dark-blue shirt. A small grease spot on the collar caught her attention; she'd noticed the stain countless times before. His khaki pants were too big for him, and the belt he wore was on too tight, making the front button fold down underneath his belt buckle. With olive skin and black hair, Wade liked to think of himself as a gift from the old country. A gold class ring with a blue sapphire was handcuffed to his pinkie.

"The kid—" Maya started.

Wade's bored expression came to life. His fuzzy caterpillar eyebrows sprang up as if they'd been caught sleeping on the job.

"Told us *nada*. We won't get another shot at him till the trial."

"Who knows when that will be," Wade said. Less of a question and more a statement stuffed with genuine melancholy.

Maya's fingers tap-danced across the keyboard again. Wade was her fellow detective, but they'd never been close. The top brass, for some reason, were infatuated with him. She couldn't understand how they could endure that in-your-face attitude he so loved to flaunt. As he walked away, Wade hummed a familiar tune: "Hush, Little Baby."

# CHAPTER 16

TUCKER SUCKED IN AIR THROUGH his teeth. The sweltering midday heat radiated through his truck, and without wind, the open window didn't offer any comfort. Still, boiling in the cab seemed better than going in there. He glanced across the gravel parking lot at the yellow light illuminating the paint-chipped sign above the entrance of Denny's Clam Shack. *How'd it come to this?* He dropped his hat on the seat and ran his stubby fingers through his hair. He closed his eyes and massaged his scalp.

He'd thought he'd hit bottom by losing his traps and his heritage, but then his boss, Bill, from Mark One Security had taken Tucker aside while he was working at the hotel and explained how their biggest client had failed to renew their contract. Bill was forced to downsize the company, and he chose to keep only the most senior security guards. He canned Tucker right then and there.

"I wouldn't be here if I had any other choice," he said. Tom Braxton had been propositioning him with promises of quick cash on and off the water since spring. As May and June progressed, his offers had transformed to threats. Soon after, Tucker's traps started disappearing, then they had a run-in where Tom aimed a revolver at Tucker's chest. Despite Tom's best efforts, Tucker had kept the fat fucker at bay. Until the fluke nor'easter blew through. Now it was the first of August, and with the traps and his livelihood gone, he could only hope Braxton's offer still existed.

During their run-in on the water, Braxton had said, "Your father would have taken this offer."

Tucker couldn't argue with that, but Dad hadn't been a saint. He'd been seedy and mean as any son of a bitch. Growing up, Tucker had learned hard lessons, taught with strict punishment. He'd taken his licks, but as he got into high school, he started to fight back. He grew muscle, stood taller than Dad. No coincidence that around that time, Dad eased off, no doubt sensing the shift of power. Tucker used to take silent pleasure in the way his looks made Dad shrivel and his barks made Dad cower. Then Dad died, and in some final act of rebellion against his stronger son, he'd left Tucker the family house. Tucker bore the overwhelming debt to spite the dead prick.

The violence in the Flynn household died with Dad. Tucker had never lifted a finger against Melanie, Jacob, or Kevin, and he never would. "Your father would have taken this offer." All the more reason why Tucker hated being there. He'd fought against the mortgage for years, but now it threatened to swallow him and his family whole. Only one way out, and it was sitting in the bar, waiting for him.

His eyes snapped open, and he rolled up his window. He put his hat back on and yelled, "Fuck!" He stepped out of the truck and slammed the door.

A cluster of bells rang as he stepped inside, and the cool air conditioning brushed his hot cheeks. He dismissed the smiling hostess with a wave. The girl nodded, quickly covered her braces with her lips, and stared at a pile of menus on her podium. No way he'd be able to afford braces for Kevin with his current income. *God knows the kid needs them.*

A boisterous crowd in the main dining room sat beneath coral chandeliers resembling white spruce trees that hung from the low ceiling by weathered marine rope. The windows offered natural light that spilled across the half-filled tables. The sounds of glasses clinking and silverware ringing off plates filled the space. A burst of laughter from a red-cheeked bald man at the booth in the back caught his attention. The guy clutched his stomach and wiped his eyes with a napkin. As Tucker continued, a young waitress cut in front of him, ferrying four piles of fried seafood from the kitchen porthole. The aroma of fish and fries lingered.

He cleared the dining room and headed to the bar at the back of the building. When the bartender, Ingrid, spotted him, her eyes bulged. She seemed to be trying to say something with her face. He held her eye contact until she pushed her tongue into her cheek, shook her head, and grabbed a rag and went to work wiping the chipped mahogany bar top. He'd dated Ingrid in high school, and after a few rocky patches, he'd dropped her and her attitude in his wake. Despite the shark teeth, she still had some of the best tits in town. Was she on the payroll? Or had she finally learned to keep her stupid trap shut?

Tucker sighed and regarded the group of men at the far right corner table. Two of the guys had their backs to him. Tom Braxton loomed over the three like a nesting bird. His ass took up half a bench. Beside him was the blocky, rugged face of Nick Turner, a lobsterman with a cut-throat reputation; he'd played chicken with Tucker more than once on the water. Tucker always backed down, because Nick wasn't just crazy, he was certifiably nuts. No way to beat a man who had no rules. He stayed out of Nick's way.

The men went quiet and gave him their attention. The other two faces came into view. Chris Flannigan, a curly-haired Irishman who Tucker had on more than one occasion thrown back a few pints of Guinness with, faced him with a weak smile. Chris put down his glass and sucked foam from his red goatee. Chris wasn't all that bad, but he got annoying as he constantly complained about his money troubles. Although the last time they'd drank together, Chris had bought the rounds and even splurged for some top-shelf whiskey. *Guess they got him too.*

"Flynn, pull up a chair. We were just talking about you," Tom bellowed across the room.

"Chris, Tom, Nick..." Tucker shook their hands and turned to the last man. "Never got your name."

The lean-bodied guy wore jeans and a black T-shirt. He'd been a "deckhand" on Braxton's boat the day Tucker had caught Tom cutting his lines.

Braxton spoke up. "Jean-Pierre, just call him JP."

Tucker offered his hand, but JP disregarded it. Tucker dragged a chair over and sat next to Chris.

JP stared at Tucker. "I... uh... assume that I do not have to tell you that since you are in, there is... uh... no leaving?" JP's accent gave him away as French Canadian, English clearly being his second language.

"Figured as much," Tucker said and rubbed his chin.

JP maintained his stare. "And if you go to the cops, well... uh... we own the police."

"I figured that too."

"And if I ask you to do something, and you refuse to do this thing, we will... uh... take your wife and son, tie them to chairs, pour gasoline on them, and... uh... light them on fire. We'll burn your house, boat, and you... uh... we won't burn you. We'll cut you" —his hand cut the table several times like a butcher's knife— "into small chunks, piece by piece, while you're still alive, and use you for... uh... lobster bait."

"I got it." Tucker rubbed the back of his neck. *Just try to hurt my family, you bastard, and I'll pound that ugly face of yours to pulp.*

Chris bumped Tucker's shoulder. "We've already got the fucking cops on our side. We're completely fucking covered." With Flannigan, it always seemed necessary to throw in a "fuck" every couple of words.

Tucker faced Flannigan. "What about the Coast Guard?"

Nick spoke up before Flannigan could. "Don't get much trouble from them." Nick offered a hollow laugh. "The fucking Canucks got our backs, and that's all you need to know, Flynn." Nick had a nervous energy about him. He hands shook as if he was over-caffeinated, and his eyes darted as if he were following an imaginary fly. Nick was unpredictable at best, and his attitude fluctuated by the minute.

Tucker glanced at JP's face, which remained deadpan.

Tom spoke up. "We've been doing this for a while. Anyone that gets between us and the money loses. You think Carl Mending jumped off the Skog Bridge because he was mental?" He smiled a split-glass smile. "This ain't the only town moving heroin, Flynn. Newborough isn't just a place it passes through — it's the destination. Small towns, they're under the radar, and we can control the law. The money's good, and all we have to do is bring the drugs in and load them into trucks. We don't know where it goes. That's not our job."

Tucker glanced at Chris, who nodded and said, "Aye, he's right, the money's damn good. Beats hauling fucking traps all day and coming home broke to an angry fucking wife, right?" Chris gestured with his half-empty pint then poured the rest of the black liquid down his throat.

*Why do I get the feeling that this is not going to end well?* "I understand. So what happens next?" Tucker said, staring at JP.

JP leaned in close. "You're going on a run tonight. Time to… uh… how you say? Get your feet wet."

# CHAPTER 17

MAYA PARKED IN FRONT OF 286 Common Avenue. The
reports had already been filed and the case closed,
but she couldn't shake the feeling that she had
missed something with the Carl Mending suicide. Wade had
written the case off as a lapse of mental health, which she didn't
disagree with. Before Carl had jumped, he yelled at Wade and
her, projecting his paranoid delusions of corrupt cops and the
conspiracy mumbo jumbo that she'd heard before. Still, the
case felt unresolved. Carl's medical history hadn't shown he
was taking any sort of psych meds. His autopsy had shown
that his blood was clear of drugs and alcohol. What drove him
to off himself? She knew men could be stubborn, so maybe he
had an undiagnosed mental illness. Sometimes the wounds you
couldn't see cut the deepest.

That was why she was adamant with James. Years of coaxing
him into anger management therapy had finally worked.
His mood had improved. The shift was au natural, no pills
whatsoever, which meant that whatever Dr. Wayneright was
saying was working. He hadn't complained about any more of
his angry episodes. She'd had some small part in him seeking
therapy. She'd told Carol about him, asked her to introduce
herself at the debriefing, and when James discreetly swiped her
card off the desk at the meeting, Maya had almost cried.

He was stepping up, for her and for their baby, as she
always knew he would. She'd typecast James when she first
met him, back when she was still a rookie cop. The "good-guy"
social worker, a man who would be a concerned lover and a

great father. He was all those things, but with a complicated, violent past.

On their first date, they'd chatted over a couple of mugs of coffee downtown then taken a barefoot stroll along the beach. While the waves engulfed their toes, she buffeted him with the questions. At one point he put his hands up and stopped her. He made a "plea bargain" to barter their personal lives, a question for a question.

"Have you ever dated a black woman before?" she'd asked.

"No, but I'll try anything once. Have you ever dated a white guy before?"

"Yes, and since I showed up, you can imagine that I'm at least a little interested."

"Do you want kids?" he asked.

"Yes, is that a deal breaker?"

"Not for someone who wants to have kids… which I do too."

She asked, "Do you have any problem with cops?"

"Nope. Do you find me attractive?"

"Ah-ha, yes, and I'll ask you the same."

"I think you're the most beautiful woman I've ever seen."

"I'm blushing, but you probably can't tell."

"I think you're smart too," he said.

"That wasn't a question."

"A question, huh. Well, how would you like to go back to my place?"

She knew he had expected her to be shocked by the question. Instead, she had responded with, "My place is closer."

286 Common Avenue. Maya glanced at the mailbox in front of the house. The metal box was spray-painted to resemble a fish. White but outlined in black, the fish was decked out with a spiked dorsal, pectoral fins, and a curled tail, all of which appeared to be hand-sculpted from wood. The yellow-eyed fish face in front of the box gasped for breath. She licked her cracked lips and peered out her window, over a moss-infested rock wall and down the S-shaped driveway to the brown house, shaded by tall oaks and maples.

Mrs. Mending opened the front door, carrying a black plastic bag. Maya turned off the engine and stepped out of the car. She strode up the driveway and caught Mrs. Mending just as she lifted the lid of a trash can and dumped the garbage.

"Hi, Mrs. Mending, I'm Maya, a detective with Newborough Police."

She dropped the plastic lid with a clatter. Her narrow shoulders sank, and she inhaled a long breath through her nose. Her face appeared ashen, and two shadows streaked under her brown eyes. She brushed several thin blond hairs out of her face and crossed her arms under her drooping breasts. "Detective Wade told me you guys were through with the investigation." Her voice was strained, as if she was trying to stave off screaming at Maya.

"I know. I just wanted to follow up with you, if you have a few moments." The soft approach was Maya's only shot at getting her to talk. The last thing this woman wanted to do was talk to another badge.

Mrs. Mending rolled her eyes and frowned. "Only if you swear to me that you won't come to my home again."

"I swear." Although that promise wouldn't prevent phone calls or having someone else come on her behalf. "I know this is a tough time."

"Sure, like you'd have any idea what it's like. Come in, let's get this over with—and call me Jen."

Jen's home was immaculate, which for a grieving family, was the last thing most people would expect. After a death, relatives and friends usually came, helped cook or clean, trying to ease the pain by doing something physical, something practical like making a casserole, washing dishes, or vacuuming the carpet—anything to avoid talking about the death, especially with suicides. Jen led Maya past the dining room, the table set with four sunflower place mats for Jen, the two daughters, and Carl. Little comforts, even placebos, protected the mind from the weight of the sorrow, if only momentarily. At some point, she'd have to put that place mat away.

In the living room, Jen pointed at the couch, and Maya sat on the right side. When her butt sank into the cushion, the light smell of musk danced in her nostrils.

"Not there, that's his place." Jen pointed at her.

Maya shot up and slid over to the center of the couch.

Jen wiped her forehead, offered a "sorry," and sat in a wooden rocking chair.

"No problem." Maya reached into her blazer pocket and pulled out a cracked moleskin notepad. She flipped to the first free page, bookmarked by her pen, and asked, "Before he died, when was the last time you saw Carl?"

"I already answered—"

"Some of this may be repetitious, but I need your help on this."

"Help with what? What more is there to know? They said he had some sort of psychotic episode, depressed, paranoid hallucinations..." Her voice rose, but she brought it back down, her pale fists clutching the arms of her rocker as if she was breaking through the atmosphere on a space shuttle.

"I know, Jen. I'm just trying to see if there's anything we're overlooking."

"Fine." She sighed. "The last time I saw my husband alive was before work in the morning, eight thirty, the day he died. He'd lost his job on the fishing trawler, so I pulled a few favors to get my old job back teaching daycare while he tried to find more work."

"Was he laid off? Fired?" Maya already knew the answer from the file. NE FISH Corp had laid him off, but what she didn't know was Jen's feelings toward her husband's job loss. Did they get into a big argument that pushed him too far?

"The owner of his company laid off the entire crew. Had some sort of 'mid-life crisis' and sold his boats and the entire business to some Canadians, so he could start some *real-estate* company down in Florida." She shook her head then stared at a row of picture frames on the mantel.

Maya followed her eyes. The biggest picture, in the middle

of the row, showed the family. Carl, dressed up like Santa, smiled with his arms holding Jen and his two daughters, both long-haired blonds like Jen. The oldest was probably ten and the youngest around five years old.

"The guy actually sent me a check."

"The old owner of the NE FISH Corp?" Maya asked.

"Yeah, said he *feels* bad. If he had *really* felt bad, he would have sent the money before Carl jumped off that bridge." She shivered. "I can't even drive over that goddamn bridge anymore. Have to drive around —"

"Jen, I never saw mention of a check from his former employer on any of the reports."

Jen frowned, and she focused on Maya's eyes, probably trying to get a read. "Didn't think it mattered. Does it?"

Maya flipped her right leg over her left and noted on her pad to research NE FISH Corp and the Canadian company they'd sold their business to. "Depends. How much was the check for?"

Jen opened her mouth, and Maya detected a slight hesitation. Maya pulled out her badge that dangled from a chain around her neck and rested it on the lapel of her gray blazer.

"Forty thousand dollars — which seems like a lot, but that's chump change for this guy, believe me." Jen's hands patted the air in front of her.

Forty thousand dollars from her dead husband's former employer, and it didn't seem worth mentioning? Or was Jen afraid it would be relevant and somehow the money would be taken away? It had to be more than a kind gesture. Bosses didn't compensate ex-employees' families just for dying. *You don't get rich by handing out money when you feel bad.* And why did he really sell his company? After she researched the deal, she would examine their books.

Maya closed her notebook and made eye contact with Jen. "Do *you* think Carl was mentally ill?"

Jen massaged her temples and shook her head. "No. Carl

was always a solid man, my anchor. He never yelled, always kept his cool." Her eyes began to take on water.

Maya stood and shook Jen's hand. Jen's palm was clammy and her grip limp. "Thank you for your time, Jen, and my condolences for your family's loss."

Jen pulled her hand away and examined her wedding ring. "I'll show you out."

# CHAPTER 18

THE SHARK PASSED SLOWLY THROUGH the water, quiet and fluid, a thick body of muscle and teeth.

"Jesus!" Maya's hand was flat across her chest. "I didn't see that coming."

James slid beside her, a broad smile parting his face. She'd fallen away from the tank only to be sucked back in again by the underwater views. Maya stuck her palm against the glass. The blue ripples of light from the tank found refuge in the diamond on her left hand. The water's glow fell across her black skin, clinging to her as if an aura of azure. Her eyes followed the schools of fish, whose flashing scales brushed by, seemingly inches from her nose.

"I love you," he whispered in her ear, his lips brushing the tiny sensitive hairs.

Maya turned and slung her bare arms around his neck. "I love you too, babe."

He felt a rush of arousal. Embracing the feeling, he lunged with his teeth bared. "Duna, duna, duna, duna duna."

"James... James!" Maya's voice rose to an urgent whisper. "Not here."

He munched on her neck. All she could do was squirm against the tank glass, half giggling and half pushing him away. James kissed her skin, leaving a trail of moist ovals. She scrunched up her face, inhaled sharply, then released a pleasure-filled exhale—music.

She fought against him—or pretended to—but when he

tickled her armpits and blew on her neck, she put force into her shoves.

"Ahem!"

When James turned around, he was greeted by two parents sporting a pair of matching indignant frowns. A couple of yardstick-tall kids tugged about their dad's pleated pants: a red-cheeked boy wearing a corduroy Red Sox hat and a girl in a blue dress.

"Sorry," Maya blurted as she squeezed out of James's grasp.

James smiled, the humor outweighing the awkwardness. Or maybe the awkwardness made it funny. Either way, the kids seemed to get it.

He was dragged away by Maya's strong grip. They walked higher up around the main tank, the heart of the New England Aquarium, conveniently built beside Boston Harbor. The central tank had the appearance of a giant test tube with a ramp that circled to the top like the threads of a humungous screw.

"You're ridiculous, you know that?"

As she spoke, James made a show of looking around, then he leaned in and mashed his lips to hers before she could continue. She kissed him back. He reached behind her back blindly, found her bra strap, pinched the clasps, and released the hooks.

"Urgh, you know I hate when you do that," she said.

"I know that face. Fine, I'll fix it."

"Thank you."

At the top of the tank, James and Maya shouldered through clusters of school kids. Together they gazed in and pointed down into the tank's depths. A large sea turtle glided across the top of the water. Its spade-shaped head poked above the surface, breaching for a quick breath. The way the light crosshatched its back made the turtle look like a living mosaic.

They walked down the ramp to the lower levels that had smaller tanks filled with exotic creatures. They passed fish that glowed in the dark and an electric eel with dead eyes. Maya stared intently at a lobster.

"You can see those at the supermarket, babe," James said.

"I know. It's funny. I've never really *looked* at a lobster before. They're like little aliens."

James got close to the glass. The armor-plated crustacean flexed its antennae, taking time to clean the length of each by passing them through its fang-like mouth. James watched curiously as the creature sucked one black bulb eye in and out of the socket. The lobster's claws were laid out in front like a bulldozer. Dark red blazed about the sides of the shell, and black splotches littered the back from tail to claws.

How was Tucker doing? He hadn't talked to Tucker since the beach, which was just over three weeks ago. James had been busy, but mostly he wanted to give Tucker time to try to fix his situation on his own. The stubborn lobsterman would never ask for help.

There was movement from behind a forest of kelp in the back: an albino lobster, layered with a tint of blue like the veins on a pale forearm. James stepped back and read the sign above the tank. "Gulf of Maine Exhibit," "American Lobster," and "Rare Blue and White Lobster." He'd lived on the New Hampshire Seacoast his entire life, and James had never once thought about how the coast of New England and parts of Canada were part of a gulf.

"Any new breaks with the drug trafficking?" James asked.

"I'm working on something." Maya stared at the lobsters.

"That all you're going to tell me?"

Maya met his stare with soft eyes. "I don't want to talk about work. This is our day, Jamesey." She grabbed his hand and laced her fingers.

"What about Amanda, if it's a girl? Amanda Morrow."

He and Maya had been toying with name ideas lately even though they wouldn't know the sex for months. Maya always guessed girl names, and he guessed boy names.

"How about we call her *Two*?"

"Two? Two... Morrow. Urgh, you're such a tool sometimes." Maya slapped his butt.

James chuckled.

Before they left, Maya wanted one last look at the penguins. They were in a big, deep exhibit at the front of the aquarium entrance, with rocks to perch on and ample room to swim below. They stunk, which came as no surprise, because if you watched their bored expressions, there was usually one shooting a stream of toothpaste-like shit out its little tuxedo body. The penguins below were more like dogs, swimming circles and chasing shadows. James didn't get the appeal.

This time James had to drag Maya away. His arm wrapped around her waist as they left the aquarium. He slid his hand down her back, past her white shirt, and crossed the border of her tights to the smooth curve of her butt. She swiped his hand away and replaced his arm back around her waist.

The cool summer night air offered the smells of the historic Boston Waterfront. The strong scent of seaweed and saltwater mixed with the damp bricks, street meat, and the invisible steam rising out of the sewers. There was no particular rush to retreat to the car and make the drive north. Instead, they walked the wharves, speaking very little.

They came upon a vacant series of columns supporting concrete arches that created a long, open corridor. As they passed through, James regarded the wooden lattice work above their heads. The sun had allowed tangles of stringy vines to weave a green roof of teardrop leaves that searched desperately for hope-filled rays. The red full moon above left the leaves wanting. Amid the greenery, white ornamental lights supplied a romantic glow that gave James goose bumps across the tops of his arms.

"That moon is huge!" James said.

"What's today…? August tenth? It's the supermoon tonight."

"Wow." James stared. It hung in the sky like a massive celestial pumpkin.

"Spare some change?" Leaning against a concrete pillar and squatting on a green camouflage blanket, the homeless man extended a tin can that clinked and rattled when he shook it. The man's clothes were covered in rips and stains, and his skin was caked in dark layers of grime. Probably in his fifties, he wore a tired face cracked with wrinkles and stubble.

James waved him away and muttered, "No, sorry."

The man latched his eyes on Maya. "Miss, you seem nice. Can you spare some change?"

Maya shook her head and frowned at the man. "I'm sorry, no."

The man grumbled something under his breath.

James led Maya down concrete steps. "Anywhere else you want to—"

"Ouch!" Maya grabbed the back of her head.

James put a hand on her shoulder. "What's wrong?" A biting pain stung his temple. He saw, at the top of the stairs, the homeless man pitching coins at them. "Hey!"

The homeless man threw a hail of coins.

Maya's hands were up, but several coins struck her face. "Ah! Damn it, this guy's nuts. James! No."

James charged up the steps as coins stung his face and chest. *He's dead. No one hurts her.* Another round of coins struck his face and chest, but he hardly felt the pain. His vision was red, his adrenaline surging, his vision tunneled. The man's twisted face grew closer with each step. His father's angry face stared at him. The homeless man threw the can and turned to run, but James leapt and tackled him, tumbling with him. The smell of feces and body odor on the man's shirt and the underlying scent of vodka assaulted his nose. The concrete scraped and jarred James's muscles and joints, but he moved quickly to stop the man from scrambling away. He shoved the man's face into the ground and flipped him around.

James mounted his torso and jabbed his fist into a face that had become his father's boiling red face. He hammered his fist down on the man's skull, emphasizing each word, "Don't. You. Ever. Touch. Her. You. Son of a bitch!"

Maya pulled him off the man, who was left dazed on his back. "James! Get off of him."

"He tried to hurt you and the baby!"

"James, calm down! I'm here. Calm down." Maya pulled him to his feet and leaned him against a column.

His jaw was locked tight. James blinked several times. The sound of blood in his ears began to fade and was replaced by car horns and the water lapping along the wharf. James exhaled like a cement truck's air brakes releasing pressure. *I blew it. I couldn't control myself. I hurt someone.*

"I think I need help." James sniffed and wiped his cheeks as tears slid down his face.

The homeless man scrambled to his feet and shuffled away, holding his head.

"We need to get out of here," James said, wincing as he flexed his right, blood-flecked fist. He stared at Maya's concerned face.

She glanced back over her shoulder through the archways, where the homeless man had taken off. "Let's go."

# CHAPTER 19

MAYA'S PALMS WERE MOIST AGAINST her cheeks. Her elbows dug into her desk, and the computer screen was blurry. She yawned and scratched her eyes. She rubbed the back of her head and probed her scalp, trying to find any mark from where the coin had struck her yesterday.

During their car ride back home from Boston, they'd talked at length. James admitted he'd lost control.

"I thought I was past this," he'd said. "I saw him hurt you, and I just lost it."

She had suggested he push for Carol to prescribe him something. He promised her he would. Maya didn't bring up the man he'd attacked again. In all honesty, the homeless man had assaulted them, and they'd defended themselves. Maya had scanned the area for witnesses, but at night and covered by the arches, no one had seen the fight. She and James wouldn't press charges, and the homeless man had taken off. There was no use dwelling on the fight.

Maya stared at the single paragraph article on her work computer screen. A Montreal-based company under the name JP had purchased NE FISH Corp. The sale appeared legitimate, but the price, $1.4 million, seemed low. No way of knowing until she got access to NE FISH Corp's books.

"NE FISH Corp?" Wade's voice bellowed inches behind her ear.

"Damn it, Wade, stop doing that!" Maya stood and faced him. Several other officers had turned in their seats.

"Sorry, it's a joke. Besides, I've always liked getting a rise out of you."

"Don't you have something else to do right now?" She tried to burn him with her eyes.

"Not really, but I'll pretend I do." He gave her a wave as if she wasn't worth his time.

Her desk phone erupted, and after three long rings, Maya lifted the phone off the cradle and clutched the speaker to her ear. Melanie Flynn was the last person she expected to hear on the other end.

---

A little before dinner time, Maya perched alone at the bar in the back of Denny's Clam Shack. The bartender, a pale-skinned woman, revealed half a foot of cleavage and several blue veins so faint that they seemed to have been drawn on her chest with colored pencil.

She slid over and spoke through a serrated smile. "Sure you don't want a drink-drink?"

"No, thanks." Maya brushed a hand through the air as though she was sweeping a fly off her food. "But I'll take another orange juice please." She rubbed her belly.

"No problem, hon." The bartender slipped the glass of orange juice on a coaster, latched her hands on her thin cheeks, and propped her elbows up like tent poles on the bar top. "Never seen you in here before."

"My first time."

"Makes sense," the bartender said and gave the empty bar a casual sweep of her eyes.

"Why does it make sense?" Maya spun the ice in her drink with the stirring straw.

"We get a rough crowd in here at night, hon. Fishermen, deck hands, those kinds of guys. They're all fat, rough, and genuine dickheads. Not many women—classy women—like you and me." She offered a heavy wink, her long lashes dusting the air.

"Actually, that's the type I've come to see—a lobsterman."

"Which one? I know 'em all." Her eyes zoomed in on Maya.

She stopped stirring her drink. "Tucker Flynn."

"I know that one—too well—unfortunately," the bartender said then rolled her eyes. "He owe you money or something? If so, get in line."

"No, nothing like that. He's just a friend of my husband's."

"Married." She seemed enthused. "Let's see the stone." The bartender spread her own ring-less hands wide and leaned closer.

Maya offered her outstretched hand.

The woman swooned and caressed the small sparkling diamond. "It's beautiful, hon."

"Thank you, he's one of the good ones. How about you?" Maya asked, surprised to find her voice shaky.

"Haven't found the right guy yet. Two divorces and three kids later, still by myself. Thank the Lord for child support."

Maya smiled on the outside and winced on the inside. She sipped her orange juice and surveyed the bar.

The bartender winked at her again and flicked the button on the little TV. Over her shoulder, the woman said, "Your secret's safe with me."

Maya cocked her head at the woman. Could she see the baby bump?

"The badge," the bartender said, pointing at the glimmer of exposed metal dangling underneath her sport coat.

Maya tucked the badge into her blouse. She'd left her Glock at home, opting to only bring her 9mm handgun, concealed in the small purse in her lap.

The bartender laughed. "You're a local celebrity." She motioned toward the TV. "Caught you on the news. You really served justice to that drug dealer. Nice going, girl!"

"Thanks." Maya put her hand to her brow. "You saw my fifteen minutes."

"Oh, don't say that, hon. I'm sure you'll find a way to get back on TV. Plenty of bad guys out there needing their asses kicked."

"Maybe you're right." *Pretty heavy on the chat, even for a bartender in an empty bar.*

"So how far along are you?" the bartender asked.

"About nine weeks. Can you really tell?"

"You're drinking orange juice at a bar, and you've been eyeing your little bump like a lap dog." The bartender had a cackling laugh.

"You should have just said I was glowing," Maya said.

"Oh, come on now. You're gorgeous—and sexy. Any man would be lucky to be with you."

*Is she hitting on me? Or is she trying to get me to say something?* New Englanders were like can openers—they cut and pried until they could see what you looked like inside.

Maya waved off her praise. "Tell me about Tucker. Seems like you know him well." Maya rested her cheeks on her hands.

"Tucker, Tucker, Tucker, well, he's a stubborn ass. Good-looking, in a redneck sort of way. He means well, but so does everybody, you know?" She plucked a random glass from a tray and gave it the once-over with a dish towel. "Tucker changed a lot when he settled down with Melanie and had their two boys." Her tone switched to solemn. "Well, one kid now, but that was a shame."

"Yeah, I heard about Jacob, but I never learned how he passed away. If you don't mind me asking, how did he die?"

She put the glass back and leaned close to Maya. "Jacob fell overboard and drowned."

"That's awful." Maya waited for more.

"I'll never forget that day. I happened to be staring out the back window over there, and I saw them walking out on the dock together. Jacob was a little younger than Kevin is now. The weather turned, and they had gone out past the Isles of Shoals to go fishing." She picked a hanging scotch whiskey glass, examined a black speck of grime, and scraped it off with her nubby nail. "I've known Tucker since grade school. We dated off and on. Back then, he was a total prick. He thought more with this head than this head." She motioned toward her crotch then her temple. "But that's another story. For as long as

I've known him, Tucker has always had shit luck, but he never deserved what happened to him that day."

She rehung the glass. "They were still out past the shoals when this crazy-assed storm blew through. From what I heard, his boat had motor problems. Big waves — I'm talking big waves — were tossing his boat all over the place, but with no motor, it might as well have been dead in the water. Tucker, being the stubborn guy he is, didn't call for a tow. He's the type to keep banging and beating away at a motor." She paused. "From what I've gathered, Jacob wasn't a strong swimmer, so why he liked being out on the water? I haven't a clue. Probably just loved to be with his dad."

*Oh, poor Tucker.*

"Tucker, knowing Jacob ain't a strong swimmer, at least had the sense to hand him a life vest once it got rough. The paper said a big wave hit them and tipped the boat damn near over." The bartender used her hands to mimic the motion of a tipping boat. "Jacob was tossed overboard."

*Oh, God.*

"Jacob hadn't fastened his life vest correctly, because when he hit the water, he sank like an anchor."

"What did Tucker do?" A heavy lump had formed in Maya's throat.

"He jumped in after him, no life vest or nothing. Problem was that he was battling big waves in a rolling sea." She shook her head. "They never found Jacob's body."

"That's awful." She wanted to say more, but no words seemed big enough to match the size of the loss.

"It is. Tucker himself was nearly lost, but another boat came, and the men pulled him out of the water, half mad and half drowned. They had to have three guys restrain him 'cause he was fighting them like a swordfish. They even went as far as knocking him out and tying him up, because he was trying to dive back into the water."

Maya cradled her stomach. "That's an incredible story."

"Yeah, poor Jacob didn't deserve that."

They were both quiet for a few moments, examining their thoughts. The TV hummed; the Red Sox were in the second inning against the Orioles.

The bartender glided over to the window. "Looks like the guys are starting to wander in now. I don't think I need to tell you that no one brings up *that* day around Tucker."

"I would assume not." Tucker must blame himself. *I don't know that I'd ever be able to recover.*

"Sorry to be such a downer, hon. What's your name again?"

"Maya."

"I'm Ingrid."

The door opened, and the first man threw up three stubby fingers and shouted with an Irish accent, "Hey, Ingey! Tree pitchers of the fucking cheap shite."

Ingrid rolled her eyes at Maya and winked before she went about filling the first pitcher.

Maya glanced over as the men passed through her peripheral vision. She recognized several faces that she'd seen that day from the dock. Colonel Bender had said, "That's Tom Braxton's boat..." Tom tested the floor with every heavy tromp of his boots. *What had Colonel Bender called his boat? The* Water Angel, *yeah, and no forgetting that pleasant face.* The man who had stared at her that day, the one with the dark features and the flat, disinterested gaze, followed Tom Braxton.

The three other men wore tattered shirts with miscellaneous construction company logos. Their trucker hats bore similar salt-stains that bled white like crashing waves. Their boots dragged, shifting the floor while the boards complained and moaned. Tucker came in last, his hands dug into his jean pockets, his eyes staring at his tan steel-toes. He wore a long-sleeve flannel shirt rolled up to the elbows. His demeanor was solitary while the other men seemed to favor the company. Chairs scraped as the men claimed their seats, several taking the time to eye Maya. She ignored their stares. The fishermen didn't even try to whisper; she could hear all their assessments.

Tucker glanced up, and when he met her eyes, his went wide

with recognition. He stopped and seemed unsure as to whether he should continue going to the table where the rest of the men congregated. Maya turned on her bar stool, and he was caught in her net.

"Hey, wow. Good to see you. You with James?" he said.

"Not tonight. I was actually hoping to speak with you."

Tucker directed his gaze back at the guys who were starting to take interest in them. "Not really the best time, to ah, well... what was it you wanted to talk about?" His voice was low.

"Take a seat." She patted the stool next to her.

"This isn't really a good place," Tucker mumbled as he sat down.

She matched his low voice. "It won't take long. The thing is, Tucker, I know you've gotten yourself mixed up in some illegal business."

He studied her for a moment, then his eyes veered away.

Before he could rebut her, Maya continued. "I got a tip from a *very* reliable source. I know your situation, Tucker. You're hurting. You reached for the quick money."

Tucker crossed his arms over the edge of the bar top. "Don't know what you're..."

Maya leaned closer. She focused on his concerned expression. "Tell you the truth, the only reason I came here is because of James. He sees something in you, and I don't want him to be disappointed. He's much more compassionate than I am. I suppose that's why I love him." She spun away and touched the condensation on her glass. The ice inside shifted, then she said, "I'm offering you a way out before I inform the cavalry and bring this whole trafficking operation down around you."

Ingrid swooped past them with three pitchers of beer clutched in her sturdy arms. She threaded past the empty tables to get to the pile of men in the back before heading toward the kitchen.

"I—" He stopped himself, winced, and made a small groan. His lips sealed, and he narrowed the space between his eyebrows. "I've never been a good liar." He scratched the back of his neck. "I'll talk, but not here, or even downtown at the police station."

"It has to be tonight. I can't stall this. Things are going to happen quickly," she whispered.

He rubbed his scruffy beard, rearranged his hat, and whispered, "Walmart. One hour. Meet me in the fishing section. I'll tell you everything I know—but me and my family will need protection."

"I'll make sure you get that protection, once you talk. I'll be waiting in the fishing section. Don't be late." Maya stepped off the stool.

"I won't," Tucker said.

"Hey, Tuck! Who's your lady friend?" The bulky fisherman clapped a bloated hand on Tucker's back and nearly knocked him off his stool.

"Eh-hey, Tom, this is my friend—" Tucker's body seemed to shrivel in the man's presence.

"Maya," she interjected.

"How you know Fucker—I mean, Tucker?" Tom smiled and put his hands on his wide hips.

"We met at a Red Sox game last month. He and his family sat right next my husband and me—third base side, great seats." *That ought to be specific enough for Mr. Nosy.*

"Sounds like it was a lot of fun," Tom said in a monotone voice.

"It was." She twisted away from Tom. "Nice bumping into you, Tucker."

"Sure you can't stay? Have a drink with us?" Tom asked.

Maya turned back to him. *Oh, I'm sure we'll be seeing each other soon, but it won't be to get a drink.* "I'm sure. I have a date with my husband."

"Oh, what a shame," Tom said.

Maya left a five on the bar and patted Tucker's shoulder as she left. She steered for the exit.

"Who'd they play?"

Maya felt the fisherman's question hit her right between the shoulder blades. She turned to face Tom, who was now leaning over the bar stool that Maya had just occupied.

"What was that?" she asked.

"The Red Sox. You said you guys went to a game last month. Who'd the Sox play?"

Tucker started to say something, but Tom silenced him with a glare.

Maya searched her brain for a likely team. "The Yankees."

"That's funny. They didn't play the Yankees in July." Tom didn't take his eyes off Maya.

"The White Sox," Tucker spit out. "Same colors, you know? Women always screw up the teams." He laughed weakly.

Tom looked back at Tucker then raised an eyebrow at Maya.

"Oh, yeah." Maya nodded then snapped her fingers and pointed at Tucker. "That's right. My husband is the real baseball fan." She giggled. "That, and one too many seven-dollar beers."

As she walked away, Tom said, "Night, Maya."

"Night." She waved then pushed through the screen door.

She closed the door behind her and berated herself for the stupid mistake. She squeezed her purse so hard that she could feel the outline of her 9mm.

She'd parked her white Audi convertible in a boat yard two blocks up the road on the off-chance that Tucker might recognize her car. She'd have to sell her Audi baby when the real baby came. A two door stick shift just wouldn't be practical. The moon was out, just shy of full, and casting a pale light against a darkening sky. She stopped and stared. Yesterday, she and James had admired the supermoon together. *I hope Carol gives him some meds today.* She continued on. The leaves of the maples surrounding the boat yard shook under a slight breeze. As she glanced at the row of large white hulls, a small animal burst through the undergrowth, bounding away from her and scaring her to the point where she put her arm to her left hip, searching for the welcome weight of the service gun that wasn't there. "Damn squirrel."

The air around her grew still, and the dark shadows of the

canopy seemed to sink. A twig cracked behind her, slicing through the silence.

She wrenched around in time to register the man in a white wife-beater tank top and ski mask swinging a dark object that crashed down on her head. A thunderous pain split her face. She fell backward. The attacker moved in on her and swung the object again. Maya couldn't see through her right eye, but her left registered the swinging crowbar. She rolled away, pushed off the dirt, and scrambled back to her feet. She'd dropped her purse—the gun. Some of her shattered teeth floated among the blood oozing in her mouth.

The attacker lifted the crowbar high and swung sideways. Maya ducked and pounced on him in his backswing. She missed with her right jab but followed with an uppercut that met jawbone. She grabbed his shirt and launched her knee into his crotch.

He grunted and stabbed her shoulder with the crowbar. The metal crushed muscle and stunned her arm. Maya grabbed her shoulder while she backed away. She yelled for help but only managed a moan, her mouth obstructed by blood and tooth fragments. He recovered and rushed her, bringing the crowbar down and across. Maya blocked with her forearm. Bone cracked and gave way to forged steel. She scrambled toward the road, but he knocked her facedown into packed dirt and weeds. He kicked her stomach. She moaned and clutched her abdomen.

Her good eye searched for something to throw. Then she caught the shine of her purse ten feet in front of her. She crawled for it—too late. He intersected her path. Standing high over her and with both hands gripping the crowbar, he brought the steel down. *Oh, Jamesey, I'm sorry.* Maya's right arm was raised, but it wasn't enough to stop the blow that ushered in total darkness.

# CHAPTER 20

A FTER HE LEFT HIS OFFICE for the day, James met with Carol Wayneright. He'd bumped up their usual therapy session in lieu of his attack on the homeless man yesterday. After describing his anger and aggression to Carol, he explained how he wanted to regain control of his emotions. He needed the anger and anxiety attacks to stop for good.

Carol listened quietly as he recounted his attack on the man, her eyebrows knitted and her lips pressed tight. When he finished, she said, "Thank you for sharing. I can see you're shaken up still. I'd like to start you out with an anti-depressant. We might need to add anti-psychotics as well, but I want to wait and see how the anti-depressants work. I don't dish out these drugs lightly, and they can have negative reactions." Carol's soft voice seemed to express her caution. She rattled off and described the litany of side effects, the most concerning being lack of sex drive.

When he exited her office, he left with the written prescription in hand. James wasted no time in handing the prescription to the Walmart pharmacy and kicking around the store for an hour until his pill bottle was filled. At eight thirty, he stepped into the condo and was surprised to discover that Maya wasn't home. *Where is she?*

He called Maya's personal cell phone and work phone multiple times and left her a slew of messages. The police station dispatcher said she'd left at five. As he moved about the condo, he noticed signs that she'd been home recently: the bathroom light left on, the washer was spinning laundry, and Maya's service gun, cuffs, and one of her two backup guns rested in the safe, which meant she had the other backup 9mm on her. She'd also taken the gun purse he'd bought her two Christmases ago, which rarely left the gun safe. *Something's not right.*

He called Sam's cell phone.

"James, what's up?"

"Hey, do you know where Maya is?"

"No, I saw her at five o'clock shift change, why?"

"I just got home, and she's not picking up my calls on either of her phones. She was here, there's laundry on, and she took her nine millimeter with her. You sure she's not doing some follow-up work somewhere or something?"

"She didn't say anything to me. You think something's up? I mean, she might just be at the gym or..."

"I already called the gym and even Goodwill—she likes to shop there. She'd let me know if she was going out. It's not adding up."

"Hold on, I'll call the police shooting range with my work phone."

"Thanks." James waited. He hadn't thought of that. She only went shooting a couple of times a year, but that would explain the gun and not answering her calls.

"No, not there. Huh," Sam said.

The sense of mystery rushed back like a wave. "It's odd, you know? I wouldn't call if I wasn't worried."

"Yeah, no, I understand, man." After a three-second pause, Sam said, "Listen, I've just got to finish up something right now, but I'll meet you at the station. Leave a note for her at the house just in case. I'm sure she's doing errands or something. You know those big box stores block out cell phone signals to keep you shopping longer."

"Yeah, okay."

Before he left, James scotch-taped a note on the door telling Maya to call him or Sam if she came back.

At the police department, the baggy-eyed officer behind the glass in the lobby stood with a grunt, shifted his belt, and leaned over to buzz James through to the station. As James trudged down the hall, he caught whiffs of burnt coffee and fresh reams of paper. The hallway led to an open room that Maya called "the arena," nothing more than two dozen gray desks, some linked together, surrounded by a perimeter of small offices and a conference room. Fluorescent light, false ceilings, drab colors, and weathered faces all helped to reinforce the cold atmosphere, which often reminded him of his own office. Instinctually, he trained his eyes on Maya's desk, finding only a vacant chair and a dark computer screen to go with the clean workspace. He scanned past several officers who were busy typing and caught sight of Sam.

Sam put down his Dunkin' Donuts paper cup, stood, and waved him over. "Hey, James, take a seat."

James crossed the room and accepted Sam's handshake, his palm still carrying heat from his coffee. James shook his head and remained standing. "We going to head out now?"

"Sure, but first, let's think where she might be." Sam slid back onto his chair.

James massaged his forehead and paced the length of Sam's desk. "Wherever she went, she drove her personal car."

"That white Audi convertible that she drove to the police picnic, right?"

"Yeah, her police car's parked at home."

Sam slowly drummed his fingers on the desk and chewed his thin bottom lip. "First thing I checked. Department vehicles all have trackers."

"It's not like her. I mean, she's anal about keeping her phones charged and on her—at all times. I've been calling them, but both go straight to voicemail, like they're out of battery or she's somewhere without a signal."

"Here's the odd thing. Her cell phones both have GPS, so I tried to find her that way. No dice. Couldn't get a traceable signal, which means the phones are out of juice or broken."

James leaned closer, holding the top of the chair with his

hands. "I don't like this. I hope I'm just being paranoid, it's just that... something feels wrong."

"Well, let's not get ahead of ourselves. It's only been, what?" Sam checked his silver wrist watch. "Four hours since she left the station. And if her phones went dead or she dropped them in the water or something..."

James hooked his thumb behind him. "Let's go out looking."

"Okay, sure, but where do you think we should start?" Sam turned his attention to Detective Wade Copley, who circled the edge of the arena. "Hey, Wade, you seen Maya tonight?"

"Do I look like a babysitter?"

Sam cleared his throat. "You remember James, her husband, right?"

Wade altered direction and sauntered over to join them. He made an obvious effort to size up James. "I remember. How you doing?"

"Be doing better if I could find my pregnant wife." James allowed a bit of his frustration to show.

"Don't worry. She's probably shopping for pacifiers."

James faced Wade. "Most stores are closed by now, and her phones are both conveniently dead."

"All right, then I got nothing. I do, however, have work to do." Wade waved them off and strode into an office.

"What an ass," Sam said under his breath.

"Forget him. Sam, should I be worried? You know, she's arrested a lot of people, probably made a few enemies..."

"It's unlikely—" Sam started.

"It's possible," James fired back.

"Listen, I'll pass it along to the on-duty patrolmen to keep their eyes out for her and her car. I'll send someone by the hospital and shopping malls. I think the best thing for you to do is to go home and wait for her. I'll call you if I hear anything, and you do the same, okay?"

James scratched his scalp then rubbed his forehead. "All right. I'll call you with her plate information."

Sam stood and offered his hand. "James, we're the police. We have her plate info."

"That's right. Okay, I'll be at home then." He shook Sam's now cool hand and slowly made his way toward the door.

Sam called, "Odds are it's nothing."

James stopped, glanced at Wade's office and saw a shadow moving behind the glazed windows, then faced Sam. "I hope you're right."

Back at home, James sat on the couch and clutched his phone. Midnight came and went, and he fought to keep his eyes open. He yawned and laid his head down. *Where is she?* Drowsiness cushioned his head, and he eventually forfeited his worried thoughts to sleep.

*Thump, thump, thump, thump.*

James's crusty eyes snapped open, but his mind moved like sap dripping down a pine tree. The sun's light seared through the gaps in the curtains. Who the hell would be knocking on his door this early? Had he locked the door? He must have. Maya! She'd probably forgotten her keys.

*Thump, thump, thump, thump!* The knocking grew louder and more insistent.

"One second. Jeez," James muttered.

Wearing jeans and a white T-shirt, he walked barefoot to the door and spied through the peephole. Sam and another uniformed officer appeared at the other end. When he opened the door, Sam's eyes were bleary and somewhat bloodshot. The other guy was new—Charlie? Something about their matching puckered faces, the queerness of their expressions...

"Find Maya?" James asked.

"We found her," Sam said.

*Whew. What a relief. But why wasn't she here?* Their expressions seemed stone-faced.

"So where is she?" James shaded his eyes from the sun.

"James, I have some bad news." The pores on Sam's cheeks and nose glistened. "I'm truly sorry to tell you this..." His tongue passed over his top lip. "A fishing boat found a body

141

in the water this morning." He paused again. "The body they found was Maya's. Maya's dead, James. I'm sorry."

"What?" James stared into Sam's eyes then focused on Charlie, whose rigid jaw and flat mouth remained unwavering. "Seriously, guys, where is she?" James laughed once and peered past them to see if she was hiding behind their black Crown Vic.

Charlie continued in the same tone — a slow, deliberate voice. "She was hit with a blunt object several times to the head."

*What? This isn't real. Where is she? Hit by a blunt object? What, what are they telling me? She's dead? Maya's dead?*

Sam put his hand on James's shoulder and sniffed through big nostrils. His dark eyes became misty, but he stared hard at James. Sam tucked in his lips and shook his head slowly. He kept his hand on James's shoulder, giving a little squeeze. Charlie examined his shoes.

Sam repeated himself. "Maya's dead, James. I'm sorry."

"She's dead?" James felt his words as they springboarded off his bottom lip, and he abruptly realized he couldn't catch his breath. His temples throbbed, his ears rang, and the blood in his body went cold. James stepped back and shook away Sam's arm. "How? She was just here yesterday..." The ringing in his ears grew louder.

Charlie turned away.

"Maya's dead, James." Sam's words were muffled. "You have to understand. She's been killed." Sam stepped closer and used his hands to emphasize his words.

"Maya's dead," James repeated the words right before his legs turned into air and his body gave in to gravity. When he came to a few moments later, the two men hauled him up by his arms and dragged him to his couch.

"Is there anyone we can call? Anyone to come be with you?" Sam asked.

"How? Who? I... no." James's stomach heaved, and he threw up. Most of the vomit was caught by his white shirt while the rest splattered onto the couch.

"Oh, man," Charlie said. He rushed away to the kitchen and came back with two handfuls of paper towels.

Having these men in his apartment, with their black polished shoes and their stiff collars, felt odd. James's head throbbed and his limbs turned to lead, but he regained control. "I can't believe what I'm hearing. It's just not right. You're telling me Maya is dead? Hit on the head and she... died?"

"James, listen to me. I promise you, we're going to be devoting all our time — day and night — to figuring out how this happened. I promise you, I'll find who's responsible," Sam said.

"Maya is dead." He felt the vomit rise up again, and he choked it down. The acid burned his throat.

Charlie ripped off two sheets of paper towels, which he handed to James. Charlie then tentatively patted at the couch.

"Who can we call, James?" Sam asked.

James didn't respond.

Sam asked again. "Who can we call?"

Only one name came to mind.

———————

James had moved, or more accurately, Sam had moved him to the clean side of the couch. Sam had called Tucker's house. While Sam and Charlie waited, Charlie asked James to confirm his whereabouts yesterday.

"Maya and I had spinach omelets yesterday morning before work. That was the last I saw her. I was in the office all day, then therapy — Carol Wayneright — and then Walmart to fill a prescription." He pointed at the unopened bag with the receipt stapled to it sitting on the island in the kitchen. "After I saw Sam at the station, I stayed here and waited. This feels... like a dream." He felt lightheaded, and his fingers were cold.

"Did you and Maya have any arguments recently?"

In a hoarse voice, James offered him a simple "No."

Sam glared at Charlie. "Hey, I know you're still green, but this is not the time for that. James is a friend." Sam's tone expressed his authority.

Charlie put his palms up and apologized.

James's throat burned, and he couldn't get away from the acrid smell of his vomit.

Tucker and Melanie just sort of appeared in front of him.

"Jesus, James. Jesus, I am so sorry, man. Jesus," Tucker said. "I don't even know what to say. What do you need, man?"

James coughed. "Water."

While Tucker fetched the water, Melanie busied herself with rags and sprays she'd found in the kitchen and set about scrubbing the vomit out of the couch. After James swallowed several gulps of water, Tucker peeled off James's wet shirt and gave him a fresh black T-shirt to wear.

Sam said, "We have to get back, see what forensics found. I'll call you soon."

James snapped, "I want to see her. I want to see my wife."

Charlie seemed to hesitate, then Sam said, "We'll be outside when you're ready."

The living room emanated a strong lemon scent. Melanie and Tucker waited and promised James they would come with him for support.

James felt weighted down by invisible stones. He sank deep into the Flynns' blue Buick's worn upholstery. Tucker followed the squad car. Before Sam and Charlie let him enter the morgue, they warned him, tried to prepare him for what he was going to see.

Still, he was anything but prepared when the examiner, who resembled Mr. Clean in a lab coat, unfolded the top part of the white sheet and revealed her corpse. James reeled away. The sight of the gray blob in front of him was too much to bear. The place smelled of blood and formaldehyde mixed with seaweed and rotten meat.

"Son of a bitch!" James said, covering his mouth with his hand.

"The water caused gasses to build up," the examiner said. He passed around a little plastic tube. "For the smell."

144

Charlie rubbed some of the greasy gel under his nose and offered some to James, which he refused.

"James, let's go," Melanie said, putting a hand on his shoulder. "We can leave, right, officers?"

Sam started to speak, but James cut him off. "No."

James couldn't think of what else to say; he just knew he needed to see her this way. She wasn't his wife anymore. Someone had killed her, thrown her perfect body into the water like trash, and she'd transformed into this. Not just her — their unborn baby, his family. He needed this moment. He felt as if giant hands were tearing him in two, but he needed to see.

James turned back slowly. The sheet respectfully covered her breasts. Her skin was puffy, bloated. The fine angles that James had loved were now shapeless masses of flesh. Maya's beautiful face — he'd spent many a night staring at all her lovely features as she'd slept — now ruined. As if an entire tree had landed on her head, then the damaged tissue had been reshaped by a night's soak. Her hair, still wet, was gathered in tangled clumps. Her neck bulged, froglike. The odor of death was powerful, mixed with a strong scent of seaweed and blood.

The smell proved too much for his twisting stomach. He ripped the smelling gel from Charlie's hand and plastered two smudges under his nostrils. "I need a moment alone with her."

"Against protocol," Charlie sputtered.

"I'm not finished working," the examiner said.

"I need a fucking minute with my family. I'm not asking!" He wasn't taking no for an answer. *Just try to stop me, any of you.*

Sam was the one who spoke. "Clear out, guys. I'll stay and make sure nothing's tampered with."

They all shuffled out, except for Sam.

James stood over Maya. How could this have happened? She was alive and with him yesterday morning. Now she was dead, the life crushed out of her. Why her? He had never put any stock in the afterlife, a skepticism that Maya had shared as well. What made us so special that we got a heaven and hell? No, when we died, the brain stopped, they buried our bodies in dirt or burned them to ash, and that was how the story ended. But that wasn't how he wanted it to end. He needed to see her alive again, whether that meant being with her on top of some puffy clouds or walking with her in an endless desert. She was his one and only, the only thing he loved.

*Who did this to you?* He brushed the twisted hair out of her face. The skin from her scalp all the way down to her nose had collapsed and sunken inward. There was a long fissure splitting into her skull. Her face was a mottled mix of red, purple, gray, and black. Dried blood clung to her broken teeth and mouth. *I'll get my answer.*

James clenched his jaw, bent down, and kissed her lips — cold, motionless dead lips. The same as Derek Fanning's.

---

After seeing Maya, Sam told James to stay home and that he would come for him soon. The lemon smell lingered. James's couch was as clean as it would ever get.

"I've got to go. Doing a fishing charter today," Tucker mumbled.

"I can stay," Melanie offered.

"It's not necessary. I'm okay. I'm fine. You've both already been so kind." James waved them away.

"Really, it's no trouble," Melanie said.

James hugged himself and sighed. "I need to grieve alone."

Melanie hesitated. "Keep your phone on. I'll call you later to check in. You've got food in the fridge."

"Thank you. Thank you," James said. "Good-bye."

From the couch, he watched as Tucker and Melanie scuttled away. Melanie stopped and gave him one final sympathetic look as she closed the door behind them.

He sat alone on the couch, staring at the wall. Time and place were no longer significant. He started grinding his teeth. He swung his arm and struck his left cheek with his fist. Stabbing pain was followed by a residual ache. Fireworks flashed before his eye. Then he slapped his right temple. In a flurry, he punched his chest and his stomach as hard as he could.

He beat his body till he was sore, then he stood. Impulse guided his feet. Maya's locked safe. The digital code—James's birthday. He typed in the numbers, and the lock released. A set of handcuffs and two guns rested on the gray felt. Several fully loaded magazines were stacked neatly while a box of bronze mushroom-top bullets peeked above their cardboard case.

He grabbed Maya's service weapon, the black Glock 19, and shoved in a magazine with his palm. The gun's action snapped back with the smoothness of a snake bite. He placed the Glock on the bureau then eyed the second gun, a 9mm Ruger compact strapped into its leather ankle holster—her backup weapon. Heavy with ammunition, he closed the door and left his home.

———————

"A fifth of Jameson. Will that be all?"

"That's all."

"It's on sale."

"Keep the change. I won't need it."

# CHAPTER 21

NOTHING'S CHANGED HERE. JAMES LICKED his wet lips. The green bottle dangled in his left hand. He took a pull and let the whiskey swish around his mouth before he swallowed. Was this how his father felt when he drank? What was in the alcohol that had made him so vicious? James had always imagined drinking his father's drink would transform him somehow. So far, all he felt was heat in his rubbery cheeks.

He'd walked into a living memory—a photograph—although the abandoned sand and gravel pit was probably as alive as the heart of Death Valley. The hills of sand and gravel were piled into pyramids that sparkled with fragments of mica. At the edges of the pit, the silent trunks of conifers watched. Termite-infested bark, half hidden by coats of needles, wardens of the wasteland being eaten from the inside.

James's numbness was interrupted by the pinching skin at his back where he'd stuffed the Glock behind his belt. He pulled the gun out and cradled it in his hand. Even though the gun was sleeping now, he could sense its power. All he needed to do was pull the trigger to wake it up.

*The only good part of me is dead.* He gazed at the dunes surrounding him. "What's left?" Tears hit the sand at his feet and were swallowed up. "I'm nothing without her. And the baby... I never got to meet my baby."

The alcohol moved through him, quickening its pace in an effort to comfort. When he glanced at the gun in his hand, he saw the dark circle staring back at him. *Is Maya in there waiting for me?* His lips quivered. Once again he was a child cowering with his finger on the trigger while his father was winding up to plant a knuckle kiss on his cheek.

James wrenched the gun away from his face and panted. How long had he been holding his breath? The sleeve of his black T-shirt wiped his wet forehead. Another pull of whiskey.

The targets he'd set up, an aluminum army of discarded beer cans, stood at attention. A motley group of shredded cylinders sat on two long, heavily pockmarked beams that somebody had lugged out here.

James hadn't changed either—the same frightened boy who had stood there decades ago. At a distance of twenty yards, he squared his shoulders, bent his elbows, and held the gun firmly. Taking his time, he slowly squeezed the slim metal trigger. The bullet exploded from the chamber and flew through the open air until it stabbed through the target like paper. The can flew off its perch and skittered away. Another pull of whiskey. What would his father say?

"Nice shot, retard."

"Thanks, Pop."

"Why can't you listen, you goddamned moron?"

"Sorry, Pop."

"She's dead, you stupid shit."

Another pull of whiskey. James focused on the next target. The can spun away with a brand new hole through the center. A smile smeared across his face. It was as if his dad was right there, somewhere past the thin curls of gun smoke. James knocked down the rest in the row in quick succession. Another pull of whiskey.

He refilled the magazine and dropped to a knee to lift up his jeans leg. The 9mm strapped above his ankle didn't have the weight and feel of the Glock, but it was meant to be concealable and for close fire. James moved up to fifteen yards and aimed. He cleared the row with one bullet left in the chamber. He examined one ripped can, the aluminum torn open and bent like a smile. The last bullet struck the can, and the smile spun around, turning into a sad face. Another pull of whiskey.

# CHAPTER 22

TUCKER RUMMAGED THROUGH HIS GARAGE and found the socket wrench buried under a pile of screw drivers. The engine was still warm as he leaned over and shoved his arm into the crack. His fingers picked up grease, and coal-black dirt scraped under his nails. The sun was relentless but not nearly as oppressive as the humidity, which clung to his skin as if he were in a rainforest. He flicked the timing belt then rubbed it, feeling for cracks. After filling up all the fluids, he patted the engine and let the hood fall like a deadfall trap. He caught his reflection in the tarnished chrome of the grill. When he bent closer, his distorted face appeared, and he angled his jaw to see the purple bruise beneath his scruffy beard. He rubbed the tender flesh. *Bitch had a hell of a punch.* He shook his head. Replacing truck parts and cleaning the garage had been a welcome distraction, but no matter how hard he tried, his mind always swung back to the same thought. *I murdered Maya.*

He cleared and organized the bench, swept the floor, returned his tools, and took a moment to admire his work. The hanging hammers and pipe wrenches gleamed in the half light. The rusted handsaws and sharper tools hung on nails just above.

The memory of her frightened face as she lay at his feet in the dirt. She'd shielded the blow, but it was useless. He'd swung with everything he had, and the steel crowbar did the rest. He never knew a person's skull could crack and shatter like that, as if he were cracking an egg. After that, he'd panicked. Did she have his DNA on her? He needed to get rid of the body. The slow current of the creek was close. He grabbed her by her ankles and dragged her all the way to the mud. The chirp of crickets and the thrum of frogs joined the thunderous roar of his heartbeat.

*The current will pull her out to sea if I'm lucky. Either way, any DNA will be washed away,* he'd thought. Her head dragged and bounced off the rocks and through the mud. He dragged her to a rocky point where the current headed out to the Skog and lifted her as if she were his brand-new bride. He hesitated then saw her face in the moonlight. He had thought her a beautiful woman, but he'd made her ugly. He heaved her as if she were a lobster trap, and her body flew toward the main channel, where the current moved fastest. After the loud splash, he searched for any watching eyes but found only distant lights of houses and docks. She sank, and he imagined the current dragging her tumbling corpse along the bottom of the creek bed.

When he had gone back to the boat yard, JP and Braxton were waiting.

JP said, "Did you take care of her?"

"It's done. Tossed her body in the river." Tucker handed Braxton the mask and bloody crowbar. "Get rid of that. It's evidence."

Braxton said, "We didn't tell you to dump the body in the creek."

"I panicked. It's fine. I tossed her in the main channel. The current will take her out to the Skog."

In the darkness, JP smiled. "Like I said, we uh... own the police. Do not worry. We'll take care of her car." He offered his hand. "You did well. You are uh... one of us."

Tucker wished he'd thrown JP and Braxton into the creek. Tucker shook JP's hand, squeezing hard.

Even after finishing a twelve-pack of beer, Tucker still hadn't found sleep. Every time he closed his eyes, he saw Maya's frightened eyes.

Maya's body had apparently floated down the creek and gotten hung up on a sandbar a mile downriver. Braxton had told him that a boater had called it in in the early morning. Hours later, the detective had called to ask Tucker to help James.

Tucker wiped the sweat tumbling down his sideburns, thinking that after another hour in this humidity, he was liable to go crazy. He headed inside to wash up and enjoy the comfort of the new air conditioner. Kevin was relaxing on the couch, his windswept surfer hair shaking under the blowing power of the A/C unit as his eyes fixated on the new Nintendo handheld Tucker had bought him.

In the kitchen, Tucker found Melanie cleaning out the fridge. "Need some help, Mel?" he asked the butt sticking out of the fridge. They'd hardly spoken since they'd left James's apartment.

"I'm fine. This thing is filthy," Melanie said.

"It's not that dirty," Tucker mumbled.

"Dirty enough," Melanie said.

Tucker shrugged, grabbed the bar of Lava soap, and washed his hands. The dirt came off, but the engine grease had to be worked out. When he was done, his fingers still felt gummy.

Tucker was on his way to their bedroom when Melanie called out from the fridge, "Are you going to do whatever it is you do for work today?"

"I am." He saw the bait and refused to bite.

"What time will you be back?"

"I'd say around eleven thirty."

"Hmm... mhm," Melanie said without even taking her head out of the fridge.

Tucker ducked into the closet and picked through folded beach towels and old VHS tapes until he got to the shoebox. He cracked the lid. "What the hell?" Staring at the hanging shirts, he muttered, "Melanie."

He started to leave the room, but he noticed the travel bag on Melanie's side of the bed. Tucker saw several pairs of clothes folded inside.

In the kitchen, Melanie had momentarily separated herself from the fridge. She held Hellmann's mayo in one hand and a jar of Vlasic pickles in the other.

"We need to talk," Tucker said.

"Not now, can't you see I'm busy?"

"No, right now!" His voice was growing louder. He felt his neck hackles begin to rise.

"About what?"

"Don't play stupid with me."

"I don't have time for this," Melanie said, putting the jars back into the fridge.

"Where is it?"

"Where is what?" Melanie asked then reached for the bottle of ketchup on the kitchen table.

Tucker stepped in her way. "The money! In the shoebox. Where is it?"

"Oh? I thought that was mine. Seeing as I'm the only person with a legitimate job in this house."

*The bitch.*

Melanie's arm reached around Tucker and went for the tub of margarine. Tucker batted the yellow container off the table.

"Well, that was smart," Melanie said, sarcasm sticking like the yellow glob on the floor.

"Melanie, I'm not playing with you. Where's the money?"

"You've got a temper problem. I'm not about to take this kind of crap from you."

She went to reach around Tucker again, and he grabbed her wrist. He held it tight, unsure of what he was going to do, only that he needed to stop her. Melanie's face curdled with displeasure, and he let her arm go.

"I think the heat's gone to your head," she said, holding her wrist. "You're a lunatic!"

"Last time I'm going to ask. Where is the money?"

Melanie walked around Tucker to her purse, opened it, and pulled out the hefty wad of hundreds. "I was going to put this in the bank so it could collect interest, which is better than leaving it hidden in a shoebox."

"It's mine," he heard himself growl.

"What's yours is mine, Tuck. We promised to share everything when we got married, remember?"

"You have no right—"

"I have every right. As long as you're keeping secrets from me, I can hide things from you."

"You want to know what I do? Is that it? You really want to know what I do?"

"I want you to be straight with me about everything," she said.

"Fine." Tucker leaned into the living room. "Kevin, Mom and I are going to make a trip to the store."

"Yeah, fine, whatever," Kevin yelled back.

Melanie gave Tucker the stinkeye as he ushered her outside. They loaded into the truck and started down the road.

When Tucker turned his truck onto the main road, Melanie faced him and said, "I told Maya that I thought you were smuggling. I told her where you'd be last night... I need you to tell me two things." She put up two fingers. "Are you transporting drugs? And did you have *anything* to do with Maya's death?"

Tucker let the questions soak in for a minute. He concentrated on driving and sighed. "You don't know what kind of pressure I'm under here."

Melanie waited.

Tucker rubbed the back of his neck. "I'm helping bring in"— he waited for three heartbeats—"heroin."

Melanie stared at him and slowly shook her head. "What about Maya?" Her tone was low.

He pulled over to the shoulder of the road and faced her. "No, I swear. She came to me. I was at the bar, with all the guys around. I told her I wanted out, and she said she'd help me if I talked—be her informant. We agreed to meet at Walmart an hour later, and she never showed. I didn't know anything about her being dead until this morning when we went to see James."

"Do you know who did it?"

Tucker slapped the steering wheel. "Could be any of 'em: the cops, the fishermen, or the guys bringing the drugs to our boats. With Maya dead, I'm screwed, babe. My chances of getting out are gone. I don't know which cops are clean. They've probably got the FBI in their pockets too. This shit's bigger than me." Tucker sighed. "They're going to cover up her death. I don't think she's the first person they've killed." He put the truck in drive and pulled back out onto the road.

"What the fuck is the matter with you?" Melanie punched his shoulder.

Tucker came to a stop sign then turned to Melanie. "Listen, I'm only doing this for us. So we can eat, live, and save the goddamned house! You think I like doing this?"

He turned right onto Lilac Avenue and entered a section of newly built suburbs. A man watering his lawn glanced up and waved. Tucker returned the courtesy. In his peripheral, he saw Melanie was shaking. She retrieved a pack of cigarettes and lit one. The smoke was sucked through the crack in the window. Melanie burned through the cigarette, flicked the butt out the window, and exchanged it for a fresh one.

"I'm so mad I can barely... speak. You..." She shook her head. "Take me home. I don't even want to look at you." Tears ran down her cheeks.

Tucker hit the steering wheel. The road ended at a cul-de-sac, where he turned the truck sharply, making rubber wail against asphalt; he started back the way he'd come.

They were quiet until Tucker parked the car at the house. He faced her and sighed. "I saw the bag. You planning on taking Kevin and leaving me?"

She said nothing. She got out of the car and slammed the door. From the driver's seat, Tucker watched her trot up the walkway and through the front door.

He found her in the bathroom, throwing toiletries into her bag.

"I don't think this is a good idea," Tucker said, putting a hand on her shoulder.

She tore away from his touch. "Don't! You put your family in harm's way. Just get out of my way." Melanie left him there.

Tucker followed her to Kevin's room, where she stuffed a duffel bag with handfuls of Kevin's clothes.

Kevin studied Tucker and Melanie. "Where are we going?"

"Grandma's first," Melanie said, eyeing Tucker as she grabbed a pair of jeans out of Kevin's drawers, "then far away from here."

"Why?" Kevin asked.

"Ask your father."

"Dad?"

Tucker walked over to Melanie and grabbed the duffel bag by the handle. "Mel, stop this, don't go to your mother's. Let's think this through..."

She wrenched away from him and slapped his face. The cheek where she'd struck him felt cold compared to the rest of his face. His body became a roaring furnace. He grabbed her shirt with his left hand and pulled her toward him. She flailed her arms in his face, and he drove his right fist into her eye.

"Calm down now!" he yelled.

Melanie lunged at Tucker to scratch his face. He threw her to the ground and pinned her down. Melanie screamed. Kevin grabbed Tucker's shoulder with both hands and tried to pull him off her. Tucker swung his right arm and sent Kevin flying into the dresser, where he crumpled to the floor.

"Kevin!" Melanie yelled, her voice sounding like a whine.

Tucker's teeth were clenched and his hands throbbed. He looked at Melanie, who was still screaming Kevin's name.

He turned to see Kevin holding his face and cowering in the corner, and Tucker felt lightheaded. He stood and stepped backward. Melanie scrambled to her feet, grabbed Kevin, and ushered him out of the room. Tucker stood alone and stared at the wood floor. He coiled his fingers and examined his red knuckles. He heard Melanie slamming the front door, then the sounds of her car starting up and going in reverse. The motor roared as she pulled away.

Tucker left the room. His head was stuffed with dark gray thunder clouds. When Tucker walked out of the house, he was met by a stare from across the street. His elderly neighbor, Alphonso, stood on his own stoop with his hands on hips. Alphonso's wrinkled face was full of condemnation.

Tucker felt another pulse of heat sting his face. "Mind your own damn business, old man." Tucker's glare sent Alphonso packing. When Tucker got into his truck, it didn't start. He felt another ripple of fire spread through his body. "Don't you try to stop me."

He sprayed igniter fluid into the air intake, hopped back into the driver's seat, punched the key into the ignition, and turned as if he was gripping skin. The spark caught, and the engine started. He tossed the spray can into the glove compartment. Tucker drove away from the house and headed for the bar. The time on the dash read three thirty.

# CHAPTER 23

T HE MOPED'S FRONT WHEEL WEAVED back and forth between the road lines. James felt as if someone else were driving Sally Jay. At a stop sign, he waited for the road to clear, and a flock of memories flew through his head. Maya's smashed lips and her warped body, Derek's pale face, his father's fists, his mother's tears. James shook his head then patted his hair. Apparently, he hadn't bothered to wear his helmet.

"Hey! Shit for brains. Hurry up already!" the man in the car behind him stuck his head out of the window and yelled. He revved his motor, and his hand made a rolling motion.

James killed his engine, put his kickstand down, walked to the driver's side of the car, and leaned his face close to the driver. "Problem?"

The man sniffed and screwed up his face. "What the hell are doing? Get away from me, you drunk bastard!"

James pulled out the Glock and rested the gun sideways on the door. "There's no need to talk like that."

The man's eyes went wide, and he held up his hands. "Whoa! Hey, man, I'm sorry. Please, put the gun away."

James examined the gun in his hand, having barely realized that he had taken it out. He frowned then said, "Get out of here."

The man hit the gas and sped away. James read the rear license plate: BEEHPPY. *What an asshole.*

James stuffed the gun back behind his belt and sat on Sally Jay. His cell phone rang in his pocket. After four rings, he picked up and said, "What?"

"James, it's Melanie. Just listen. Tucker's got himself mixed up with some bad people. They're trafficking heroin. The cops are involved. Tucker says the police are going to cover up Maya's murder. Tucker met with her last night. I told her where to meet him, I'm sorry. Tucker said she was his only chance to get out, but someone involved killed her. Every night, Tucker meets with these men. He'll probably be heading out with his boat tonight. I've left town with Kevin—things are bad. I'm so sorry this has happened to you, I should have never told Maya, but Tucker needed her help. I never thought they would... I know if I were you, I'd want to know."

James breathed heavily and digested her words.

"Are you still there, James?"

"Yeah." James touched the gun at his back. "Whatever happens, when this is all over, get ahold of someone in the FBI and tell them what you know. I... I'm on my way to see my family." James threw the cell phone into a ditch, twisted the throttle, and accelerated, making the rear tire fishtail in a patch of sand. The moped caught enough of the road to stay upright but just barely.

He crossed a grated bridge stretching over a section of Crooked Creek. The grating made his small tires pitch left and right, creating a dull moan. James took the next left and noticed his arms felt incredibly loose, as if they'd given up working. He could barely feel his own grip. In a panic, he blew past Denny's parking lot. He tried to correct himself and jettisoned headlong into the gangly trees and thick brush. His arms and legs tangled in front of him as he tumbled over his handlebars and ricocheted off the wrist-thick tree trunks, getting scratched and clawed by every branch on the way down.

His eyes opened slowly. *Still alive.* His face was lying in a pile of rotting wet leaves. He spit out dirt that stuck to his gums. A copper taste filled his mouth; he licked the chunk of his cheek that he'd bitten into. His heart was beating in his head; warmth trickled into his left eye. He vaguely remembered knocking his head especially hard on a branch. James stood, dazed but still functioning. Sally Jay was lying on its side; the engine was off, flooded no doubt. When James picked up the moped, pain stabbed his left shoulder. He propped the thrashed vehicle against a bush. Fortunately, the bottle of Jameson stashed under the seat was still intact. He patted the wound on his head; it was tender. Despite his crash into the brush, this was where he wanted to be.

He stumbled to the edge of the trees and crested a bluff overlooking Crooked Creek and the backside of Denny's. Squinting hard, he saw that the *Periwinkle* was docked. He washed off his face and hands at the water's edge. The cold brackish water slipped through his hair and over his clammy skin.

James left the woods and strolled down the dock in his dirt-stained blue jeans. The bottle of whiskey was safely tucked into the armpit of his blood-stained black T-shirt. The humid air stuck to his skin, making the creases of his body run slick with sweat.

He nodded at a man in his boat, bent over a saw. The man finished the cut and set the board down to pat his dripping face with a red handkerchief. He brushed a glistening hand over gray work pants, raking sawdust off himself. The man watched James but made no effort to nod back.

The *Periwinkle* sat quietly toward the end of the dock. James stepped aboard as if he belonged there, headed into the wheelhouse, and opened the rectangular door to the hold. The inside was essentially a small cave stuffed with piles of gear and leftover bait. He inhaled deeply, crouched low, and crawled in headfirst.

He was met with darkness and an overwhelming odor of festering fish—his father's smell. He closed the door and groped around to get to the back of the hold. James crawled over half-empty greased buckets, buoys, shifty life vests, and large coils of rope. His hand fell into one of the buckets, and his arm slipped into a pile of warm, scaly fish. When he pulled his hand out, it was spackled with fish guts and smelled foul. At the back corner, he sat, sliding his back against the wall. The gun scraped the whole way down with him. He immediately lifted himself up as a pool of filthy water seeped into his jeans. James swore and bumped his head on the low ceiling. His hand groped until he found a bucket to sit on. He turned it over, and as he did, fish bodies splashed out, bringing a powerful odor of guts. Bent over double wasn't comfortable either, so he built a nest out of coiled rope and buoys. The stench only seemed to get worse.

James sweated as if he were in a sauna; there was no light or fresh air, save for a pinprick in the ceiling that revealed a solitary ray of sun. He choked on the rotting fish smell, and he sensed it seeping into his skin. He endured this belly of a whale, the hot stink, the dripping bloody water, and the darkness.

How had he come to this? In the gloom, it took him considerable effort to remember. Maya's death was a fresh wound. Someone had taken her from him... and the baby.

"What the fuck's the matter with you, James?"

His father's words in his own mouth. James punched his jaw. He'd have to temper his body, become hard. James banged his head on the fiberglass siding and pulled his hair. He put pressure on his head wound. It stung then radiated pain the harder he pushed.

"You can't hurt me." James slapped his face. "No one can hurt me."

He clubbed his bad rib. A spear of pain rang through his body. He clubbed the rib again, fresh stabbing fire. Another hit, the bone creaked. Hastily, he unscrewed the cap off the Jameson bottle, took three long pulls in rapid succession, and clutched the bottle to his chest. Within moments, the alcohol met his stomach and began a festering of its own. The tiny pinprick of light above him—such small hope for a man trapped in hell.

# CHAPTER 24

T UCKER STOPPED AT A POOL hall and mulled over a half-dozen pints of beer before he arrived at Denny's. He glanced through the window as he walked by, and Ingrid glared at him. Tucker waved half-halfheartedly, and she crossed her arms under her big tits. *What's her problem?*

The restaurant was packed, and the docks were full of lingering boaters, reluctant to leave the water, content to just sit, drink, and swat at the first hail of mosquitoes. Tucker stepped aboard the *Periwinkle*. She started up strong for him.

"That's a good girl." He untied the lines and led the boat out into the creek. The sun was four fingers away from touching the western horizon. The boats he passed, like him, had their dull lights glowing.

The *Periwinkle* passed under the singing bridge. A car above him sped over the grate, causing a humming sound. Tucker cleared the jetties. A few diehard fishermen clung to the sides of the channel, as if they were anemones casting their tendril lines, hoping to catch a passing fish. The lighthouse to his far left flickered as it swung an invisible beam over the choppy seas. He started to make wake and let the *Periwinkle*'s bow rise. Some of the gear in the hold tumbled around. He really ought to go through and clean it, he thought, picturing the mess. Away from the Newborough Harbor, he angled northeast, toward the Isles of Shoals. On flat seas, he could usually make a short run of it, but choppier waters like today made for rough slogging. Soon enough, he passed the small cluster of islands, some occupied while others were more or less abandoned.

As he drove, the motor's strain mixed with the sound of the ocean spray. There were no other boats in sight. He glanced at the sun at his back. It appeared like an orange, its peels melting into the horizon. The crash of something being thrown around in the hold drew his attention away from the wheel. He slowed the boat and flipped the lever to neutral. Tucker bent to open the hold door, and he jumped back when something forced its way out.

Tucker stepped away and watched as James Morrow struggled to stand. "What the hell?"

"Hell? Hell?" James swayed and chuckled as he said the word over and over.

"Yes, hell, like what the hell do you think you're doing?"

An empty bottle of Jameson hung from his left hand. Tucker searched for answers in James's face. His normally calm eyes squinted and had a glaze about them. James smelled like a bait bucket. He was soaked, and his clothes were filthy. An open wound wept on his forehead.

James crooked his pointer finger at Tucker. "You know. I know that you know."

"You're drunk and being stupid, James." Tucker stepped forward, and James reached a hand behind his back and pulled out a handgun. "Whoa there. Whoa there. Why do you have that?" Tucker strove to hide his fear behind a thin curtain of calm.

James's words stumbled out. "Just sit, I mean—stay there—I mean it. One more step and…"

Tucker stood still. He thought about bull-rushing James and knocking him over the side. There was the fishing gaff. No chance—it was on James's side of the boat. Tucker saw the lever was still in neutral. He could dive and push it forward. The jolt might be enough to make James lose his balance.

James must have caught the look. Tucker watched as James stared at the throttle for a long moment. Then, with the gun aimed at Tucker's chest, James snatched the boat key out of the ignition and clumsily pocketed it. The engine cut away, and Tucker was left with the sounds of the elements and his pounding heart.

Tucker was barely aware that his arms were raised, showing James his open palms. "Hey, let's just talk this out, buddy. What is it that I know?"

A gunshot rang out. The barrel hung in the air, where James had shot a round into the clouds. The dull echoes faded fast.

"Everything... everything! You know it all, Tucker. I thought you were my friend. You killed Maya. You killed my family!" As James yelled, froth gathered at the corners of his lips. His rabid eyes were open wide; red marks lined the creases where his lids met.

Tucker lowered his voice and spoke slowly. "James. James, listen to me. I didn't kill Maya. I swear on my family." Tucker turned his head away, flinching as James leveled the barrel and shoved the gun closer to Tucker's face.

"Better start talking, you son of a bitch."

"I was desperate, man. They were going to take away my home, my father's house," Tucker said.

"I don't care about your fucking house. Who killed Maya? Tell me!"

"I don't know. James, please just listen. I needed the money. The drug traffickers are who you want. I've only done it a few times. My family needed the money."

"Tucker, I'm only going to ask you one more time. If you don't answer me, I'm going to shoot a bullet through your head." James stumbled over his words.

"These two Canadian guys. I'm on my way to meet them right now. They're the ones who wanted her dead."

James wiped the gun over his face as if it were a handkerchief.

Tucker took advantage of the pause. "James, your emotions are out of whack, and the liquor's screwed up your brain."

"Shut up. Did you meet with Maya the night she was murdered?"

Tucker stopped the lie before it made it past his lips. If James had stowed away in Tucker's boat, he had to have talked with someone. Had Melanie told him? "I met her at Denny's. Melanie told her about the drugs and that I'd be at the bar. Maya was going to help me out of this mess. 'Cause I'm your friend, she said. She agreed to meet me later that night. I waited for hours, but she never showed."

James held the gun, his hand shaking.

Tucker needed to distance himself from her death. "The cops in Maya's department are involved. They're getting paid off to provide cover. The fishermen, like me, just bring the drugs into Newborough. The drugs are coming from these Canadians."

James spit on the deck. "This whole thing smells of shit, Tucker, and the shit is all around you." James used the gun to make circular motions toward Tucker.

"I just brought the drugs into town. That's all I did, James, I swear."

"That's all you did? That makes you innocent? I gave CPR to a boy who overdosed on the drugs you brought in. A kid your son probably knew. On top of that, you were the last person to see Maya alive. How's that for fucking innocent? 'All you did.' You make me sick."

James spat again, and the phlegm hit the deck in front of Tucker's boots. Tucker eyed the wad of red mucus. James's nose spilled a line of blood. He put his hand up to plug up the nostril. It didn't stop the flow.

"Damn it!" James lifted his nose, taking his eyes off Tucker for a moment.

Tucker lunged at James without hesitation. The gun went off right next to his face, and Tucker grabbed his ears. The deafening explosion slammed into his eardrums and left them ringing. He could taste the gun powder in the air. His leg burned, and a patch of blood spread from a bullet hole in his thigh.

Tucker cried out, hit the deck, and rolled, clutching his leg. "You shot me. I can't believe you shot me!" He stared up at James. Blood and bits of pulpy flesh splattered on the deck.

James ripped a piece off his own shirt and used it to mop up his bloody nose. He held the cloth and looked at Tucker. "That was your own fault. Were you trying to kill me too? I ought to finish you right here."

"I'm sorry. I want to live." Tucker was weeping. He wrapped his hands around his leg to put pressure on the wound, but blood spilled past his fingers. Tucker peeled off his own T-shirt and wrapped it tight around his thigh. Waves of nausea hit him as if he were seasick for the first time in his life. "James, look at us. We're the good guys. The bad guys are out there killing and selling drugs. We're their fucking puppets, man. You're doing them a favor by shooting me. You want that, James? What would Maya think?"

James threw the bit of cloth away and swung the gun in front of Tucker's face, so close he could feel its heat. "You shut up. You shut up!"

He couldn't shut up. "The Canadians are a few more miles out. Just follow the GPS heading. You'll find them waiting. They're the ones responsible for Maya's death. Check the bait. The dope's in the mackerel. They stuff the heroin in bags and shove as much as they can in the fish."

"Give me their names."

"Of who? The Canadians? The fishermen? The police?"

"I want all their names," James said.

The lobstermen, he knew. He told James how they got together at the Denny's and sat in the bar every night. Any guy in that circle was involved. He didn't know which cops were in on it, but he told him about the Canadians, JP and Marc. James sniffed and scratched his scalp.

A wave of nausea passed through Tucker's body, and he shook off a chill. "Hey, I'm starting to get lightheaded here, James. You want to bring me b-back now? I'm going to need... to get to a hospital... s-soon." His breathing was ragged.

"Sorry, Tucker, no can do."

"Come on, James, I told you everything I know. J-just let me go. You d-don't need me." His body was frigid.

"You were involved, Tucker. Anyone involved with Maya's death is guilty." James paused then said, "Jump overboard."

"What? Are you crazy?" Tucker's mind scrambled for a way out.

James's face was flat and emotionless. "Maybe I am. Jump overboard, or I'll shoot you right here. This time it won't be your leg." James leveled the gun, took aim at Tucker's face, and slid his finger onto the trigger.

Tucker grabbed hold of the rail and lifted himself up with his good leg. "I don't deserve this." He gazed at the swells below him. From there, he could just make out the Isles of Shoals, a black smear against the rim of the ocean. Tucker looked over his shoulder at James's glassy, bloodshot eyes. "I'll never make it, James. Think of my family... please." His tone was somber, his words slow and pleading.

"Shut up! One more word and I shoot, so help me." The gun shook in James's hand, and his jaw clenched. "If you make it, consider yourself lucky. If you die, then it's your own damn fault."

"I ain't never been lucky." Tucker lifted his injured leg over the other side of the rail.

"Wait," James said. "Have you beat Kevin?"

Tucker felt his stomach crush. How could James know? He thought about how he'd knocked Kevin into the dresser. He'd been so angry at Melanie and everyone laying claim to him. Tucker didn't even control his own life anymore. He'd snapped and, for the first time, put his hands on Melanie and Kevin. He'd turned into his father. A wife-beater. A child abuser. *I'm sorry, Melanie. I'm sorry, Kevin.* "Yes."

James shook his head. "You deserve this more than anyone."

Tucker turned away from James, the shame hurting more than the hole in his leg. He heaved himself off the edge of his own boat. No life preserver, weak from the loss of blood, he felt the cold water pass through his clothes and brush over his skin. Instead of feeling cleansed, he felt shock. He had to work through the pain of kicking off his heavy work boots as he treaded the choppy water. His leg throbbed. He concentrated on breathing and keeping his head above the waves.

Behind him was the familiar sound of his boat motor starting up. He turned and saw James in the *Periwinkle's* wheelhouse, his back to Tucker. James didn't look back as he pushed down the lever and steered the boat away, plowing to where the Canadians would be waiting. Fear stole into Tucker's mind. He paddled weakly with his arms and kicked with his good leg.

The sea lashed at his face and sought his mouth. Giving in to the ocean's weight would be too easy. The water wanted him, wanted to take him, as it had stolen Jacob, poor Jacob. Tucker fought the sea. He didn't want to die—didn't want to leave his family—all alone. If he could make it to the Isles of Shoals, he had a chance. He would be a good man, the best father, the best husband; he would never put a hand on Melanie or Kevin again. Make up for everything. Start a new life somewhere far away, somewhere without oceans and drugs.

With each passing wave, the stretch of islands became visible then was gone. It seemed an impossible distance. He took a breath, paddled with his arms, and kicked with his good leg. As long as he could see the islands ahead of him, he would be all right, he could save himself. He coached himself, trying to control the crippling fear. *Don't give in. Come on now. Breathe! Stroke, kick, breathe. Keep looking, it's right there. Breathe, stroke, kick. Focus! Breathe then stroke, then kick.* Hardly even felt the pain in the leg now. *Breathe, stroke, kick. Focus! Damn it. Focus now! Breathe then kick. No! Stroke! Breathe. Focus! Come on, focus! Focus! Breathe...*

# CHAPTER 25

AMES'S MIND CONJURED UP THE image of Maya's lifeless body spread out on the examiner's table. Barbs of hate again enveloped him. The small GPS in Tucker's wheelhouse indicated he was heading in the right direction. When he seemed to be getting closer to the coordinates, a white sport boat came into view. Continuing in the boat's direction, he slowed to observe the occupants. A man at the back had a pair of binoculars fixed to his face. Then there was a thick guy at the wheel. The blast from an air horn welcomed James. He returned the greeting with a single blow of the *Periwinkle's* horn.

*This is for Maya.* James ground his teeth. He pushed the lever down and aimed the bow dead center. With no plan and no thought, he followed his single impulse. The *Periwinkle* rode high in the waves. Her prow sliced through the water like an axe head. The lean dark-featured man at the back let his binoculars hang over his chest as he motioned for James to slow down. The wind whipped, and the motor whined. The drug boat's driver must have read James's intentions, because he moved to start his boat. At a boat-length away, James recognized the sudden mix of confusion and anger in his foe's eyes. James ducked his head and held on tight to the wheel. The *Periwinkle* broke through their side with a sickening crash and passed over the driver's soft body. The boat's momentum carried it across to the other side, where the *Periwinkle* hit water, pitched, and miraculously righted itself.

The *Periwinkle's* fiberglass prow had been crunched and had folded inward. The engine was silent. The sport boat was on its side and taking on water. Chunks of fiberglass, life vests, and debris bobbed in the water. The driver was gone. The other man's head breached the surface. He was splashing and coughing up water. James tried the motor, which hesitated several times before it agreed to turn over. He steered the boat, which now listed heavy to the right, through the debris, stalking the survivor as he swam back to his sinking vessel. White buckets were open and spilling loads of mackerel into the water.

The man was calling out the name Marc. James put the *Periwinkle* in neutral and went to the side. The man tried to swim away from James. James's eyes searched inside his boat and landed on the long gaff pole. He swung the shaft like a bat, and the hook sank into the man's side, so deep James could hardly see it.

That spawned a fit of screaming. "Oh, *tu batard*! Oh, ah!" He winced and screamed in French. The man shook, trying to get the hook out, which only prompted fresh screams. "*Arret! Arret!* Oh, stop, stop, stop."

James spun the man around with the pole and brought them face to face. James felt the hook end wriggle underneath the man's skin.

"Stop struggling!" James yelled.

He refused to listen.

James pulled out the gun and aimed. "Calm down, or I'll shoot."

The gun in his face was enough to make him stop. The man grabbed the side of the *Periwinkle*. He nodded and grunted. James regarded the trickling line of blood leaking out of the man's side and into the water.

"A woman was killed—Detective Maya Morrow. Who killed her?"

The man frowned as he said, "I don't know."

James twisted the gaff. The hook grated against the man's ribs, making his eyes and mouth gape. He wailed and, amid a flurry of splashing, tried to grab the shaft of the gaff in an effort to stop the twisting.

"What's your name?" James hollered above the man's cries.

The man grabbed hold of the *Periwinkle's* railing again. "JP."

"Okay, JP, every time you lie to me, I'm going to twist. So tell me everything you know about Maya, the detective who was killed."

"I heard about her in the news." JP breathed hard, spitting water past his dark facial hair.

James made as if to wriggle the gaff again.

"No. No. The lobstermen talked about her. They were happy she was dead."

James turned the pole again, twisting the hook.

He screamed for James to stop. He yelled, "The police and the fishermen were worried about her. Then she died... uh, and they stopped worrying. That's all I know. Get this out of me!"

A splash came from behind the boat. James glanced over and saw sleek bodies cruising between the floating buckets, snatching mackerel and eating them whole—dogfish. Several of the small sharks had appeared. They brushed past JP, curious about the source of fresh blood. JP yelped and twisted. James struggled to hold the gaff. Now dozens of dogfish had gathered.

"It's all that mackerel, all that drug-filled mackerel," James said. "Going to work them into a frenzy, JP."

"Please, let me up!"

The dogfish weren't big, only around three to four feet, but a school had gathered.

"Where are you from, JP?"

"Quebec."

"Is that where the drugs are coming from?"

"Yes, yes! Please, please, I never hurt anybody," he said. "I have uh... a wife and child. This is my job. Please."

James chuckled dryly. "It's never anybody's fault. The woman who was killed was *my wife*. She was carrying *my child*. Then because of your drugs, she got killed. You hurt someone, all right. Me. You hurt everyone who used your damn drugs. Because of *you*, my family is dead."

A dogfish eyed JP, rammed into him, and latched onto his bloody side. The shark shook him for a moment then let go. JP fought back. More of his blood seeped into the water. The school of dogfish writhed around him, feasting on mackerel and investigating the bloody Canadian. The surface splashed with their tails and dorsal fins.

JP screamed and splashed as he fought the sharks off, pleading with James. He grabbed the boat railing and struggled to lift himself out of the water. James kicked his face when it appeared over the rail, and JP fell backward into the water, taking the gaff with him. JP fell headlong on top of several thrashing sharks. James pushed the boat into gear and began to drive away. JP's bestial screams chased after him. When James had cleared the frenzy, he stared back to where JP still splashed.

James shook his head and turned the boat around, skimming past the flailing man. He pulled out the Glock, and when JP's head bobbed up James shot him as if he were an aluminum can. The air caught a pink mist. JP sank and was gone, lost in an underworld of dark lithe bodies.

The *Periwinkle's* steering was off. The propeller didn't seem to give him as much power as before. There was at least one leak somewhere in the hull. James flipped on the bilge pump to slow the water. He avoided pushing the boat too hard.

The damaged *Periwinkle* limped back toward Newborough Harbor. He licked his dry lips and focused on one thing. *Maya's dead*. He pictured her generous lips, bowing in the middle to release a smile. Her eyes played above a scrunched-up nose. She was so relaxed, so alive, in his head. He held the image and was horrified as her eyes changed to the dead-fish eyes that he'd seen on the autopsy table. *Maya's dead. She'll never be in my arms again*. James felt as if he'd woken up to find someone had amputated his right arm. The fact that he still didn't know who killed her haunted him.

His pulse pounded in his ears. The fishermen and the cops... that was why he was still there, to find Maya's killer. Tucker had told him how to find the fishermen. They would be next. He'd go to their bar and wait. He'd get them to spill the truth one way or another.

James was surprised to glance up and find that the shore was so close. He searched out the dark harbor. The water in the boat was now above his ankles, and the boat was losing power. James tightened his grip on the wheel and made it to the mouth of the channel, where he looped around the jetty and speared the boat onto the sandy beach at Smith's Cove. The *Periwinkle* slid several feet onto the shore and came to a rest. He stepped off the bow, and his sneakers sunk into the sand.

A single fisherman at the end of the jetty turned away from his rod to give James a queer look. James glared, and the fisherman spun his head back to face the fishing rod between his legs.

A wave of fatigue enveloped him. James sat in the sand and tried to remember the way Maya's face moved. He imagined her warm body sitting alongside him as he lay on his back, sand soaking through his clothes. He peered up at the sky. Stars watched him. He touched his cheek. The cold fingers were his. The scent of fresh blood drifted into his nostrils. His body went slack, his senses faded, and his eyes closed.

When he opened them, it was still night. His body became tense. He glanced at the jetty, but the lone fisherman was gone.

"We've been looking for you." The voice came from behind him.

James's breath caught in his throat. His eyes connected to the man standing not a dozen feet away. "Wade?"

"You got it." Wade appeared satisfied with himself.

James scrambled to his feet. Wade seemed calm, not coming closer or calling for backup; instead, he seemed contemplative.

"What do you want?" James asked.

"You. Isn't it obvious?" Wade said.

"What for?"

"You've been making a mess for me and the boys. Can't say it's all your fault, Maya getting killed and all. We let you off the chain so you could wash your mouth out with buckshot. Guess we figured you wrong." Wade scanned the beach. "Where's Tucker hiding anyways?"

James stepped closer to him. He would try a bluff. "I know all about your part in the heroin trafficking. Tucker said you're the one who killed Maya." James focused on Wade's face. There was no visible change, and he gave no reply. James pressed him harder. "What was it like killing a fellow cop?"

"I didn't kill Maya," Wade said flatly.

Wade hadn't denied the drug connection. James felt the frustration growing in his head. It tickled his fingers. He shifted his waist to feel the gun rub against his back. "You're a liar, Wade. Tell me, what was it like? How'd it make you feel, huh? Killing a pregnant woman."

"Couldn't tell you, haven't killed any women," Wade said. "Enough of this shit. Where's Tucker?"

"Go fuck yourself!"

Wade shrugged. "That's okay. You'll talk." Wade quickly pulled a weapon and fired before James could pull his own gun.

A pair of barbs imbedded into James's chest, and electricity rippled through him, dropping him straight to the ground. When the pain stopped, he looked up to see Wade standing over him. His face was calm. James was too slow to stop the black shoe that smashed down, shutting his eyes and mind to the world.

# CHAPTER 26

BREATHE, BREATHE. THE WATER WANTED to pull Tucker down. He felt so heavy. How easy it would be to give in, to let the deep cradle him like a babe. The ocean wanted another Flynn, but he fought for his life. Tucker could see the islands, see salvation. *Breathe, breathe, come on.*

He didn't find himself hating James for leaving him. That was done, in the past, but the future was there, on those islands. Smuttynose Island was connected by a rock causeway to Cedar Island and the inhabited Star Island. His life, if he could save it, was there. Melanie and Kevin waited for him, if he could only keep swimming, keep breathing.

He tried to direct his thoughts, to distract himself from the numbness that threatened to take him prisoner, threatened to stop his swimming altogether. He should never have helped them bring in the drugs. He'd been desperate. Besides, he had never made so much money in his life. The work was easy — the cops, and marine patrol, and everyone who needed to be had already been paid off. All he'd had to do was be the delivery boy. Easy, until Jean-Pierre and Braxton told him his full job description: kill Maya, the detective who was getting too close. They'd threatened to murder Kevin. Kidnap him and pump him full of heroin — another sad story of a kid overdosing. The choice was his, JP said — Maya or Kevin. This is where his decision had led him.

Once again, his mind played out the event as Braxton handed him the mask and crowbar from his truck. Tucker followed

Maya out of the bar, and after a short scuffle, he beat her head in until she lay dead.

Tucker breathed, and a wave collided with his mouth, forcing water down his throat. The sudden shock made him kick and paddle in a flurry. Had to focus, had to survive, or it was all for nothing. The island was close, but his vision began to gray. He could make out the dark shapes of rocks on the shore.

Tucker's eyes closed, and he found it almost impossible to reawaken his senses. His swimming slowed. His mind wandered. The memory of James's furious face struck him like a punch to the mouth. Tucker's limbs went slack, and his mind followed. The ocean came for him, and Tucker took the water on just as the wave lifted his body and threw him on the rocks.

# CHAPTER 27

J AMES CAME TO AS HIS face bounced off the thin, scratchy carpet of what must have been a car trunk. His wrists were cuffed behind him, and his ankles were taped together with duct tape. More tape covered his mouth. His head pounded as if he had sprung a hill on his scalp. He was alive—a truly remarkable development. Why had Wade spared him? What further use could James be?

The car slowed then stopped. The driver, whom he assumed was Wade, got out of the car. He didn't come back to open the trunk. James wriggled his backside. He no longer felt the weight of Maya's Glock. James rubbed his calves together. Wade had missed the small gun strapped just above James's ankle. He flapped his knees and tried to break the duct tape wrapped around his ankles. No good. He couldn't get to the gun from his pant leg.

James knocked his head against metal, causing an explosion of pain as lights danced across his vision. He grunted. First he needed to get his hands in front of him. Rolling sideways into the fetal position, he pulled his cuffed hands down as far as he could and tucked his legs as high as possible. He grunted as he shimmied the cuffs past his shoes. Once he had his hands in front of him, his fingers went to work on his belt, then the button and zipper of his pants. James pushed the jeans down as far as he could and sat halfway up to get his hands down his leg. He was able to pull out the 9mm, put the safety on, and hide the gun in his boxer briefs. Wade's voice, accompanied by others, was outside the car. James hurried to pull his pants up and

177

shook the car as he bounced. He zipped up the fly, buttoned the button, and was working the belt when the trunk door opened.

"Interrupting something?" Wade said with a joyless grin.

"Mmph," James's muffled voice said.

Wade ripped the tape off his mouth.

James narrowed his eyes and finished the belt. "I've got to take a shit." It wasn't a lie. Stomach cramps had been building, and his bowels were primed. He doubted they'd let him have a potty break.

"Not in my trunk. Help me lift him, guys." Wade slapped the tape back on James's mouth.

Two men were with Wade. One of them was Charlie, and the other one James recognized as the Fish and Game officer that had cited Tucker—Colonel Bender. James glared at Charlie, who avoided his eyes. All three of them hoisted James out and carried him like pallbearers. James searched his surroundings, trying to get a fix on his location. The car was at the end of a long, freshly paved private driveway, which led to a small bridge. The driveway was lit by white lampposts leading up to a cul-de-sac filled with several trucks and police cruisers. A long farmer's porch with twin rockers spread across the front of the mansion, which was three stories high with a four-car garage. The house's property was set against a thick wood of conifers. There were no other houses in shouting distance. The men carried James through the garage.

"One day I'll have *my* own island," Wade said to Charlie.

They shuffled past a narrow corridor created by a Land Rover SUV and the garage wall, filled with organized tools and a workbench. Twin Harley Davidson motorcycles, jet skis, and a Porsche rested in the other bays. Everything was well-kept and tidy. The men moved around an oil stain, which had been covered up with a layer of kitty litter, on the concrete floor. James thought about struggling but didn't see the point. His best chance would be the 9mm. These men, being law enforcement, would probably be armed. He needed to surprise them, all of them.

Wade regarded Charlie. "Don't look so sour, Chuck. He's

a bad dude. Tried pulling a gun on me." Wade brandished the Glock.

Once inside, they carried James down a set of stairs to a basement. The basement was finished, and the scent of cigar smoke became prevalent. Forest-green carpet covered the space, and brown leather furniture was spread about the room. Pictures, small antique cars, and golfing memorabilia lined the walls. They dropped James on the carpet and sat at a red-felted card table, alongside the waiting figure of Police Chief Gary McCourt. The men picked up their beers and examined James.

They appeared unsure of themselves, except McCourt, who said, "Where'd you find him, Wade?"

"That little beach at Smith's Cove."

"No shit?" the chief said, shuffling a deck of cards. "Smells like the bottom of a chum bucket."

Wade nodded. "He had Maya's gun on him."

"Good, this is good," the chief said, cutting the worn card deck in half.

"So what's the plan, Chief?" Wade asked, leaning back in his chair.

"I'm working on it. Whatever we figure has to be done tonight. Any more time goes by, and the story gets too loose."

"He's convinced that I killed Maya, by the way," Wade said then stared at James. "I sure as hell didn't like the black broad, but I wouldn't have killed her."

"Yeah, that is a mystery, isn't it?" the chief said in a melancholy voice.

"Can we pin it on him?" Wade asked, his hitched thumb indicating James.

"Maybe. What about Tucker?" the chief asked.

"His boat was there at the beach. It's smashed up in the front. James wouldn't tell me where Tucker was holding up, so I let him ride the lightning." Wade smiled then got up and poked James with his shoe. "Isn't that right?"

Even if his mouth hadn't been taped, James wouldn't have given Wade the satisfaction of a reply.

The upstairs door opened, and a pair of boots started down the wooden steps. The man had a shirt that read Marine Patrol. He was the same man who had given James a ticket for driving Tucker's boat without a license—Officer Stevens.

He stared at James and asked, "Who's this guy?"

The men gathered around the poker table turned their attention to the newcomer.

The chief spoke up. "James Morrow, Maya's husband—pay him no mind. He's in time-out."

"O-kay?" Stevens said skeptically, stepping around James. "I lost radio contact with Jean-Pierre's boat. I don't know where the hell they are. Still no sign of Tucker. It's wicked dark, and I don't appreciate playing hide-and-go-seek with him in the freaking puckerbrush."

"You take care of Tucker's boat?" the chief asked.

"Hauled it back to his slip at Denny's. The boat's still floating, just barely though."

"Anyone see you?" the chief asked.

"No one."

"You positive?" the chief pressed.

"Positive. There were no other boats on the water between the beach there and Denny's."

"Good. Take a seat," the chief said then sucked on his cigar. He exhaled a few puffs of smoke. "I think I'm getting a handle on this. Correct me if I'm wrong, Mr. Morrow. So James here wants to find out who killed his woman. Let's say he figures out she went to meet with Tucker the night she was murdered. Reasonably, he wants to have a stern talk with him. Am I right, Boy Scout?"

James tried to burn him with his eyes. He thought about shooting him right there, but he needed to hear this, needed to know who was responsible.

"So James goes and meets Tucker, or somehow goes out with him on the boat—haven't quite figured that part out. Maybe he had Tucker at gunpoint? How many bullets were discharged out of her gun?"

180

Wade released the magazine and examined it closely. "There's three bullets missing, Chief."

The chief stared at the ceiling, calculating. "Okay, so he shoots and kills Tucker, and maybe tosses him overboard. Three shots seems a bit excessive, but he's no marksman. Probably made a sloppy mess of it." The chief rubbed his cigar out in an ashtray. "This takes care of Tucker, and if it doesn't, then we will. You said it was dark out there, so James probably smashed the boat off some rocks then parked Tucker's leaking tub at Smith's Cove. Am I right or am I right, James?"

"Mmph."

The chief tossed up his hand. "Wade, take the tape off his mouth. Wife's at Denny's for my nephew's twenty-first birthday party on the decks—where *I* should be right now. No one will hear him if he yells."

Wade ripped the tape off violently. James puckered his lips against the pain.

"Well, am I right, James?" the chief asked.

"Dead wrong," James said. "What do you do for a living again?"

The chief turned back to Charlie. "I think I pretty much have this right. He's just being brave." McCourt faced James again. "Which is really stupid, because as far as I see it, you're going to be painted as the bad guy when this is all over."

They created the whole conspiracy with pen and paper. They pinned Maya's murder on Tucker and Tucker's murder on James. Then they discussed a timeline, making Wade the hero. They would take James back to Smith's Cove and recreate the scene in which he fired a gun at Wade and Wade stunned him with a department-issued Taser. Then James would manage to lift Maya's gun, and Wade would finish the job and take James out. They planned out who would arrive on scene and what each of their roles would be. They went over it over several times, figuring in all the factors.

The chief stood. "All right, let's all help Wade get Mr.

Morrow outside. I've got to get to my nephew's party before the little pissant pukes all over my restaurant. I'll get the doors."

All four men picked James up, carried him back up the stairs, and headed out the door that led to the garage. In the garage, the big SUV and the wall created a narrow space for the men to shuffle through—James had noticed it when they carried him inside earlier. The garage door squealed as metal rollers turned and the folding panels clattered. He didn't have much time; he needed to get out of their hands. He thought of Derek Fanning—when James had tried to get the boys to open the stall door, the red-haired Hanson boy had claimed he was shitting.

James released the contents of his bowels. The smell was almost immediate, but for good measure, he let them know. "Oh, God, I'm shitting myself. I'm shitting!"

The men groaned in disgust and dropped him to the concrete. James hit the ground with a thump and crawled away on his hands and knees.

The chief came up to them. "What the hell is going on? Why'd you drop him?"

"He's shitting his pants. I'm not holding the nasty fucker while he's shitting," Wade said, his face filled with revulsion.

"Well, don't let him get away," the chief said.

"Where's he going to go? Won't get far crawling on his belly like a fucking worm, and we can smell him a mile away," Wade said with a sneer.

James made it to the edge of the garage, pushed himself up to his knees, fished the gun out of his pants, switched off the safety, and faced them. The men froze in place like statues at the Louvre. Their faces permanently stenciled into his memory.

"You stupid shit, Wade, you left a gun on him!" the chief blurted.

The big SUV created a narrow shooting gallery with no place to hide, no time to run. Five cans were in front of him. He made his shots count. Charlie and Colonel Bender were stupefied as each sprouted a hole between their eyes. The third, the Marine Patrol officer, turned to run only to find the SUV blocking his way. James shot him in the back twice. Wasn't sportsmanlike, but there you go. James missed Wade, who was quick enough to duck. Wade managed to pull his gun out but not before he caught two bullets through the chest. The chief, at the back of the pack, made it to the door before James zipped two rounds through his neck, producing a small geyser of blood. The chief fell, his body tumbling down the wooden steps with all the grace of a sack of potatoes.

James remained on his knees, waiting for a few moments, not trusting it was over. A small moan brought him back to the ready. Wade shifted his shoulders but didn't attempt to rise. James pushed off the ground and managed to stand. Using the garage wall to steady himself, he hopped over to Wade while shit ran down his legs.

"Help me," Wade said, choking on foaming blood. The two weeping holes in his chest oozed with each breath.

"Who killed her, Wade?"

"Never... told me. Help me, please." He spoke between gasps.

"No problem." James pulled the trigger at point blank range. The bullet made a mess.

James used a saw blade from the tool rack to cut the tape that bound his feet. He found handcuff keys in Wade's left pocket. The cuffs clattered on the concrete floor and settled in a pool of Wade's dark blood. James closed the garage door, sealing him in with the dead. The smell coming from his pants was still strong. Instinct told him to run away from this place, yet an odd comfort had settled over him, and he smothered the side of him that proposed doubt.

In the bathroom, he hesitated only a moment before stripping and brushing aside the curtain to take a hot shower. He let the scalding water purify his skin. Moving about the house, as if he were an invited guest while his hosts were out, was an odd experience.

Merely out of necessity, he climbed the stairs to find the chief's room. He needed clean clothes. James fumbled through the dead man's dresser drawers. He settled on khaki pants that were too wide at the waist, which he got to stay up by snaking a brown woven belt through its loops. A white T-shirt, with the subtle smell of old skin and aftershave, came from one of the top drawers. Then James put on a navy-blue Hawaiian shirt, with light-blue palm trees, because why the hell not? He found a tan fedora with a black band that fit his head well enough. He slid on a new pair of socks and navy-and-white Docksides shoes that were one size too small. When he got back to the garage, he stared at the five dead men. Blood smeared the concrete, and the sulfur smell of gunpowder lingered in the air. Their bodies lay in awkward poses, some on top of each other, like a Twister tournament in Hell.

James relieved Wade's corpse of Maya's gun. He stepped over the bodies, being careful to avoid the blood. Who would be the first person to discover the dead men? Probably the chief's wife. The smell would be awful.

He stood by the garage door. *What next? Should I cover my tracks? Add a layer to the confusion? Maybe burn the house down? Yes, burn it all. That's the best bet here.*

*Let it burn, James,* his dad's voice invaded his thoughts. *The bodies, the house, and the lies. Burn 'em to hell.*

How does someone go about burning down a house? James stopped. The garage carried whispers of dead air like the halls of a mausoleum. He tapped his foot on the concrete to fill the room with sound. Then he saw the propane tank. He glanced at Maya's gun. Yes, that could work. The other thing he needed was open flame. Open flame with a bullet and a propane tank. It would probably help to have a big bullet. The police cars had shotguns. He used Charlie's keys and retrieved a shotgun from a squad car. There were slugs already loaded. *Perfect.*

He found a lighter among the tools. Once he had gathered the lighter, propane tank, and shotgun, he started doubting himself. Was this the right idea? The fire would bring the rest of the police down on his head. Then again, tomorrow, people would start to wonder where five of the town's uniforms were. What to do next? James studied the supplies. A homemade bomb, really. Tucker had said the fishermen always met at the bar in Denny's Clam Shack for late-night drinks. He'd bring his bomb to the bar. Take them all out in one swoop.

# CHAPTER 28

J AMES PARKED CHARLIE'S POLICE CAR behind a copse of pines in the vacant land across the street from Denny's Clam Shack. He listened as the police scanner crackled and squawked about traffic stops: a drunk driver, another car with expired registration and inspection, disorderly conduct, a man with a warrant out of Texas. The rest was undiscernible information buried under a pile of police codes. Nothing that indicated the bodies had been discovered.

James peered at his reflection in the rearview. A tired, hollow-looking set of scarecrow eyes stared back. He would have to pay for the lives he'd stolen, but not before he got the fishermen. *I miss you so much, Maya.*

The parking lot was still full, even though it was late. As he approached from the right side, he saw dozens of party-goers on the back decks while others lingered about the docks. They'd set up a bar outside, and a throng of young men and red-faced adults yelled and laughed over the music. He circled to the back and spied the *Periwinkle* docked at her usual spot, as if the night had only been a nightmare. But the damage to her hull and the water on her deck promised him he wouldn't be waking up from this.

Inside, James passed the busy dining room and made for the back bar. He tilted his fedora down and sat on the only available stool. The bartender, a big-breasted flat-faced woman, asked him what he wanted. When she spoke, he saw a flash of icicle teeth, reminding him of a shark, reminding him of JP, reminding him of the things he had done. He pinched the bridge of his nose and closed his eyes. His bad rib radiated pain whenever he moved. The cut on his scalp from the moped accident beat with his pulse, and his tender eye throbbed from when Wade had knocked him out at Smith's Cove. No doubt about it, he was starting to feel the hurt.

"Double shot of Jameson," he said.

She poured him the shot and collected his cash. After she made change, she moved on to another customer's drink order. James brought the whiskey close to his nose and breathed in the woody and caramel aromas. In the mirror behind the multicolored liquor bottles, he saw the three fishermen clustered at the table behind him. One of them, a triple-extra-large-sized guy, still wore his fishing bib. The men seemed to be brooding over their beers. They spoke in hushed tones that James strained to hear.

"They weren't there. I waited, circled around a bit, but they never showed."

"Something ain't right," the overweight fisherman said.

A newcomer brushed right past James and joined the table of fishermen. He spoke in an urgent whisper, and the men leaned in to hear what he had to say. James could only make out a scattering of words spoken with a thick Irish accent.

"Shot up... fucking Chief's house... all of 'em... who could have..."

James threw the shot down his throat and walked out of Denny's. The night air cooled his skin, and goose bumps appeared on his arms. This would be how it all ended. James's face felt as if it must be smiling. He took his time and crossed the street.

He saw the shotgun, lighter, and propane tank on the cruiser's passenger seat. His pulse sped up. James closed his eyes and embraced the adrenaline. He put the shotgun under his right elbow, stuck the lighter in his right pocket, and held the full propane tank in his left hand. James walked away from the police car. At the edge of the road, he waited for the traffic to clear. Cars drove past him, completely unaffected by and unaware of anything outside their windows. Denny's was on a bend, so the fast-moving cars coming down the road appeared then disappeared in an instant.

A police car appeared, driving at a solid clip. James froze as he stared right into the cop's eyes. The cop's eyes popped wide with recognition. *Sam, old buddy, old pal.*

Sam hit the brakes and threw on the lights. He was out of the car in what seemed a microsecond, gun drawn. "James, throw down your weapon!"

James could hardly believe the speed in which his plans had changed. "They're in there, listen, Sam. I need to finish this for Maya."

"Think about what you're doing, James. I miss her too, man, but you can't bring Maya back."

"If I go in there, I can get all of them. They deserve this." James took a step out onto the road.

"Stop! Don't. I *will* shoot you."

"No, you won't. You want to see these scumbags pay just as much as I do. One of the guys in there killed her." James tried another couple steps.

"You don't know that." Beads of sweat appeared on Sam's forehead.

"You have no idea what I know. These are the drug traffickers. They're guilty, Sam!"

"James, don't make me do this."

"I'm going to go in there, Sam. I'm sorry."

James started running. As he reached the other side of the road, he grew confident that Sam had made the right—pain. So much pain in his side. The sound of the second gunshot let him know that the first bullet had company as another punched through his back. James stumbled face-first. The propane tank rolled away from him, and his arms went slack. He lay with his face on the gravel. He coughed blood and struggled to crane his head up. The entrance to Denny's was within twenty yards. The people inside had stepped out: lobstermen, drunken partiers, and the restaurant staff. James felt their confusion. He'd been so close. Now the pain growing from his back and his side were stealing his life.

Sam's voice drained away in the background. "Ambulance... Denny's Clam Shack."

His final thought before he closed his eyes and waited for death to take him away was that he'd failed her.

# CHAPTER 29

J AMES SAW MAYA, ALIVE AND in reach. She grabbed him and kissed him. James's tears flowed, and he kissed her back. His lungs felt as light as balloons. They were together again. She stepped back then turned away. He stared at her through bars. The bars of a lobster trap. He pleaded with her for help, but she kept walking, deaf to his pleas. His arms and legs were caught, and he struggled against invisible bonds. The pain grew, and he shrieked against the burning in his back and side. "Come back!"

"Mr. Morrow! Calm down, you're going to rip your stitches."

James opened his eyes and saw the frowning face of a nurse. "Am I... alive?"

The nurse's gloved hand pressed down on his shoulder. "Yes, you're alive." She was short and squat and wore scrubs that had moons and stars printed all over the blue fabric. She let go of him and placed the plastic tip of a thermometer in James's ear. "One hundred and one... your temp is going down." She had plump rosy cheeks and a long chin.

"Where am I?" James asked.

"Newborough Hospital ICU."

James tried to lift his arms but found resistance. "Why am I tied up?" White padded straps latched around his wrists and ankles, tethering his limbs to the bed.

"Why don't you try to rest, Mr. Morrow?" the nurse said, backing out of the room.

She'd dismissed him with a simple deflection, but he was too tired to call her out on it. From his position, James examined the bandages where the bullets had passed through. They'd hooked him up to multiple IV fluid bags. A pulse oximeter, taped to his finger, transferred his heartbeat to a monitor. He tried to lift himself up, but pain engulfed his chest and side. The screen beeped and lit up red. The number spiked above one hundred for a moment then dropped back down. He gasped for breath and stared at the ceiling.

"Hey, honey." Maya slipped into his vision as her heels echoed off the floor. Her hand held the bedrail to his right. Her face was smooth and her smile generous. She wore a blue suit with her gun strapped to her hip, as if she were at work.

"Maya." Tears dripped down his cheeks. He wanted to hold her, to kiss her, but the damn restraints held him to the bed.

Her fingers combed through his hair then her palm cupped his cheek. "Don't cry, Jamesey. I love you."

"I love you so much," he coughed the words, his lips wet with saliva and tears.

She smiled above him, her eyes calm.

"You're not" — he sniffed — "you're not really here, are you?"

"What do you think?" She tilted her head and concentrated her brown eyes on his.

"I think you're a hallucination, like Derek Fanning."

"Funny you mention him."

"Hey, Mr. Jay, what's good?" Derek came to the left side of James's bed. A pair of headphones wrapped around his neck, his brown hair falling below his face like a weeping willow.

"I don't know these days, Derek."

"You wife's a cool *chica*."

James eyed Maya, who giggled. "You hear that? I'm cool."

"You're a pussy, James, a scared little pussy." At the end of the bed stood his father. His brown-stained teeth flashed for a minute. He swigged from a green whiskey bottle then wiped his grizzled chin with his red-and-black flannel shirt sleeve after exhaling a long, "Ah." He read the bottle's label then focused one eye on James. "Jameson. James-son. Ha! Get it?"

"Get out of here, dad."

"I'll go when I please, James."

"Ignore him," Maya said.

"Yeah, that's the right play, eh? Boy's been ignoring me his whole life, and this is where it got him — tied up in a hospital with nobody alive left who cares a lick about him. Ignoring me was the stupidest thing you ever did, boy."

"I'll take care of this prick." Tucker walked into his field of vision.

His father laughed at Tucker. "What are you going to do about it? You're the same as me!"

Tucker peered down at his cracked hands. "I may be the same as you, but I know how to deal with my kind, and James isn't like us. He's a good guy."

Tucker put James's dad in a headlock. His father yelled and swore, but Tucker hauled him out of the hospital room.

"Good riddance," Maya said.

"I'm sorry, Maya," James said.

"It wasn't your fault, Jamesey. None of this was your fault."

James couldn't wipe his tears. "I should have seen this coming. I wasn't even there to bury you, for Christ's sake." He turned his attention to Derek's curious pale face. "And Derek, I didn't pay close enough attention. I could have helped you too."

"I was always going to do what I did, Mr. Jay. It was always going to go the way it went."

James sniffed to keep the mucous at bay. "I don't believe that. I could have saved you both."

The monitor beeped, and Maya and Derek turned to face the screen.

"Jamesey, I will always love you." She kissed his forehead, her lips cold against clammy skin.

Derek patted James's forearm. "See you around, Mr. Jay."

James screamed and wailed. His back and side radiated a stabbing pain. Derek faded and was gone like an exhaled breath in winter. James turned to Maya. Her smile melted, and her face became long and filled with sorrow.

"Pushing Ativan." The frowning nurse had taken Maya's

place at his side, and she injected the drugs into the tube attached to his arm.

He fought his restraints, only making the pain worse, and then... then he was floating. Weightless, as if he'd fallen into a pool. His arms and legs drifted, and he became wrapped in peace. *Maya.*

When he came down from the high and could feel the bed, his aching joints, the bullet wounds, and the restraints again, he embraced the true depth of his sorrow as if someone had laid a kettlebell on his chest. The nurse slid the glass door open. She was accompanied by a doctor, a middle-aged man with beady eyes. James glimpsed a police officer seated outside the glass door. Sam. The doctor and nurse moved as one to James's bedside. The nurse handed the doctor the charts.

"How do I look, Doc?" James asked. "Will I be able to play the piano when I get out of here?"

The doctor gave him a scrutinizing stare and said nothing. He seemed annoyed at having to be in the room. "Blood pressure is still low. Fever has gone down, and the other vitals have stabilized." The man brandished a pen light and shot the yellow glare into James's left eye. He then moved the light to the right eye. "Are you still seeing hallucinations?"

"Not right now, unless you're one."

"Fortunately, I'm the real deal, which means the anti-psychotics are doing their job."

Carol had mentioned putting him on anti-psychotics just days ago. Although judging by his beard, James doubted it had only been a few days. The doctor wordlessly examined James's wounds. He told the nurse to change the dressings, handed her the clipboard, and started out of the room.

James called after him, "So I'll be okay then?"

He stopped but didn't turn around. "You'll live." With that, he continued out the sliding glass door and into the hall. The nurse remained.

"What's his problem?" James asked.

The nurse chewed her lip as she changed his dressings. "I

don't know that it's my place to say, but you should probably know. One of the men you killed, the Chief of Police, was a friend of the doctor's."

"Oh."

He'd left a pile of bodies in his wake. They'd all had family and friends who would be left to feel the hurt. Maybe it would have been better for everyone if Sam's bullets had hit his head. The nurse offered no more conversation.

Lunch came with a male nurse wearing black scrubs. He spoon-fed James different-colored versions of mush and gruel. Once he was done, the nurse left, and Sam slid through the door before it closed.

"I've been thinking of what to say to you," Sam said.

"And?"

"I've still got nothing." Sam tossed up his hands and let them fall to his sides as he took a seat across from James's bed.

"You shot me."

"I did." Sam rubbed his knees as if they bothered him.

"I could have gone in and taken out a pack of drug trafficking murderers all at once."

"You forget there were innocent people in there too. I don't regret shooting you, James. Maya would have done the same to protect bystanders from becoming collateral damage. To protect you from... you."

"What do you want?" James asked. *Come to finish the job?*

"You have any idea on how long you've been out?"

"A week?" A blind guess.

"Two weeks."

"What's it matter anyways?" With the four-point restraints, James felt as though he was on display. It irritated him to not have control of his body.

"The good news or the bad news?" Sam offered.

*Everything will be bad news from here on out.* "Maya's still dead, right?"

"She is," Sam said, bowing his head in respect.

"You find her killer?"

"Not yet, but we're investigating."

After all this, how had no one figured out who'd killed her? The not knowing was enough to drive James insane, even though, all things considered, he probably was.

"Then there really is no good news." James turned his head away from Sam.

"The *good news* is that you brought Internal Affairs and FBI into Newborough. They investigated the case and determined that the officers you killed were all involved in trafficking heroin into New Hampshire. In fact, the DEA exposed a drug network all along the east coast. Dope's coming in from Quebec. They're still putting the pieces together, but because of you, they're now investigating it."

"What happened to the fishermen?" James asked.

"There have been arrests. Everyone at the bar was taken in for questioning. Had you blown them up, we wouldn't have been able to extract the information we did."

He'd been so close. "It would have been one hell of a show though." James stared at the ceiling and plastered on a fake smile.

"It would have been murder." Sam's voice went cold.

"Aren't I already convicted of that?"

"From what the FBI has figured out, it seems like there's a good shot at calling what you did at the chief's house self-defense."

"Really?" James had a tough time believing that.

Sam leaned forward in his chair and rubbed his hands together slowly. "Charlie's squad car's camera was aimed right into the garage. We saw the whole thing go down."

"Wow."

"Maya teach you to shoot like that?" Sam asked as he leaned back.

"My old man." James balanced the new information in his head. Sam had said nothing about JP and the other Canadian he'd killed. What of their deaths? They had been a ways out, and the boat, their bodies, and all evidence of their existence had sunk into deep waters. Maybe no one would miss them?

"Ready for the bad news?" Sam's tone grew more serious.

"No, but go ahead."

Sam folded his hands. "Tucker Flynn's body was found, washed up on the rocks of Smuttynose Island."

James examined his fingers.

"He died of exposure and blood loss. The local islanders freaked." Sam stopped, apparently waiting for a reaction.

James observed Sam's flat expression for any hint of accusation.

Sam avoided eye contact and continued. "The gunshot to his leg was linked back to Maya's gun, which you had in your possession. They're going to try to charge you with the murder of Tucker Flynn on top of attempted murder at Denny's. Now, no one knows what happened out on the water with Tucker. Your story will be the majority of the evidence. This is the part where I recommend you get yourself a good lawyer."

James's head ached; the whole thing gave him a sour taste in his mouth. He released a big sigh. "Was Maya taken care of, Sam?"

"She was given a full police funeral. With you missing and no close relatives around, they bent the rules and let the department take care of the arrangements. I volunteered for the task. She was buried in a nice plot under a maple tree."

Sam's words gave him some relief. Maya had been put to rest by a friend they both trusted. *Thank God for Sam.* "I never expected to survive all this. Do you think she hates me, Sam? I've screwed so much up."

"Hell, I don't know. What's the difference?" Sam said. He slumped in the chair and echoed James's sigh.

James wanted to cover his face with his hands, but the restraints held him like pins in a frog dissection. Sam got up to leave. When would he be able to talk to Sam like this again? Maybe never. He needed Sam to know he was still a friend to him and Maya.

James choked out, "Thank you."

Sam stopped and faced James, his face solemn and his eyes

focused. "Maya was like a sister to me. I know she would have wanted me to protect you." Sam stepped out and sat back down on the chair outside, leaving James alone to cry.

The next day, a different officer was on duty. The nurses came and went, as did James's meals. Would they take him to prison once he was well enough to leave? No one told him. They treated him as if he were a bag of trash no one wanted to handle. Maybe they would give him the death penalty? Put needles into his arm and put him down like a dog. They would never let him back into society again. They didn't release rabid dogs back into the population. He examined his restraints. His hands, his legs were no longer his to command. He'd lost Maya; he'd lost his freedom. His body was the body of a murderer. The kids from the rec center... how did they see him now? Those days seemed so distant, but their faces came to him. He'd betrayed their trust. James knew how it felt to be betrayed by the people who were supposed to protect you, the good guys.

James had finished his lunch when the officer on duty came in and told him he had visitors. Melanie Flynn nudged into the room, holding Kevin's hand. The boy's eyes darted as if he expected something in the room to fall on him. The officer stayed in the room, sitting in the chair by the door.

Melanie tentatively approached James, her face blanched ivory, as if she had no blood left to spare. Frizzy unkempt hair stuck out every direction. The sight of her overwhelmed him. They stood at the end of his bed and stared at him with matching sleep-deprived eyes.

"I don't know why I came here," she said.

James nodded. He didn't even try to think of anything to say.

"They told us that you've been charged with Tuck's murder." The words seemed to drain the life out of her. "I want to know the truth."

"You deserve to know the truth." James glanced at the police officer. "Can you give us a minute?"

The officer had muscular biceps that ballooned at the edge of his short sleeves when he folded his arms. He didn't seem to own a neck. "Can't, I've got orders," he said in a deep voice. Melanie's body shook as if she were a whistling tea kettle dancing on a stovetop. She moved to James's side, considered the restraints, and made sure to keep Kevin behind her. "Whisper it to me," she said.

James told her the truth, a gift only he could give her. Telling her made it seem real, instead of an alcohol-induced dream. The hardest part was telling her how he'd forced Tucker at gunpoint to jump into the ocean. James wanted to apologize, but he knew it for the useless thing it would be. Sorry wouldn't give her a husband or give her boy a father.

She backed away to the foot of the bed and held Kevin again. Melanie patted her frizzy hair with her hands. She seized a breath and blew out a shaky exhale. When she moved to leave, she hesitated. "Tucker wasn't the perfect husband. He wasn't the perfect father..." She seemed lost, staring at her son for almost a minute.

Kevin glanced at his mother through pink puffy eyes that matched his lips.

"Tucker took out a large life insurance policy on himself. I think... I think he knew." That was all she was able to say. Tears spilled out of her eyes like an overflowing glass of water.

She wiped them away with her thumb, and she and Kevin hurried out of the room. The officer resumed his watch outside the door.

# CHAPTER 30

JAMES WAS DISCHARGED FROM THE hospital then detained without bail until the trial. He spent his days in the cells of a detention center in Concord. They kept him separate from the rest of the prisoners due to his healing wounds and weakened condition. He hired a lawyer, Joanne Keats, whom he'd heard was good, and he met with her regularly. She told him that the state was scrambling for evidence that he had murdered Tucker.

Joanne went on about how the case had attracted a frenzy of media and gained national attention. Apparently people had started calling him "The New Smuttynose Murderer." Superstitious locals told stories of how the spirit of Louis Wagner, the dead murderer, had come back and inhabited James's body. He was the bogeyman reborn.

Not that he would, but Joanne told him not to speak to the media. He told her everything, every detail. Joanne spoke in spurts and scribbled pages of notes. She didn't seem afraid of him. It was actually the opposite — the woman intimidated him. Joanne seemed too quick and smart, as if she were already a step ahead of him. James bided his time until the trial began. He kept to himself, mostly because there was no one to talk to besides Joanne and prison guards.

The day of the trial dawned. He didn't feel right in his own skin, let alone wearing a suit from the man he used to be. His white shirt smelled like his fabric softener, and he donned the baby-blue silk tie that Maya had bought him years ago. The clothes were his, but they didn't fit anymore.

The state prosecutor put Melanie on the stand. She appeared extremely fragile, but her hair was put together and her face had a little more color, probably courtesy of Maybelline. She told the court about the phone call she'd made to James and about the last time she'd seen Tucker alive. The prosecutor fleshed out the friendship that James and Tucker had shared. None of it was substantial. The major evidence was the match of the bullet wound in Tucker's leg to Maya's gun.

James was moved by Melanie's fragile poise. She kept herself together, even when Joanne asked her about the life insurance money that she'd received for Tucker's death. James hadn't mentioned that to Joanne, but she had somehow dug up the information.

Melanie glanced at James, her face full of hurt at another betrayal. James gave her a look that he hoped said, "I didn't tell her." His lawyer explained that Tucker may have killed himself to absolve his family of debt. Melanie didn't utter a word about what James had told her in the hospital. That made him go from queasy to wondering if he could keep down his food.

The prosecution requested to show the police video of James killing the officers at the chief's home. Joanne was in a small rage over that, saying how James wasn't being charged with that incident because it had already been proven as self-defense. The prosecutor argued that the footage was merely a way to show James's character and his effectiveness with a weapon. The judge allowed it but only played the video for the jury, the lawyers, and James back in his chambers. James watched the video as if he were watching someone else. The shadowy shapes of his captors were alive again, carrying him. They dropped him, and James crawled toward the entrance of the garage. He watched himself get up to his knees and shoot the handgun. The muzzle flashes flared. The men were screaming and dying. When the video was over, Joanne observed James, probably expecting a reaction, though she herself showed none. James could only wonder what she truly thought of him.

Joanne called Carol Wayneright, his former psychiatrist,

to the stand, something else they had never discussed during their conferences.

Confident and comfortable would be the best two words to describe Carol's appearance. She was dressed in a sharp business suit jacket over a coral-pink blouse and a knee-high matching skirt. She wore just enough makeup to accent her features but not cover up her flaws. Carol took the oath and strutted across the courtroom floor as if she were the teacher and everyone in the courtroom were her students. Her presence put him at ease, although he had no idea what she would say.

Joanne asked Carol to describe her professional relationship with James and dug further into their conversations during their therapy sessions.

"James comes from a history of family abuse. Maya was a strong source of support for him." Carol took a deep breath. "It's my medical opinion that James has been dealing with depression, resulting from his history of abuse. He also described multiple occasions where he suffered from panic attacks. At our last session, I prescribed him anti-depressants, which I'd hoped would be a start to helping him cope with his anxiety. James also was afflicted with hallucinations and symptoms related to paranoid schizophrenia. Now, I didn't meet with James enough to properly diagnose him, and that doesn't excuse his violent acts. Every day, people with mental illnesses live normal, healthy lives. I believe, over the years, James had developed control over his psyche through his own mental strength. I was working with him to understand his painful memories."

She went on to say, "The trauma of losing Maya—in my professional opinion—was the catalyst that bent his mind to give in to feelings of retribution." Carol shook her finger at the jury. "It can't be overlooked that in his family, there is a history of alcoholism. From the case reports I've read, there was a significant presence of alcohol in James's system when he was taken into custody. That would have caused his depression to worsen, potentially creating hallucinations and a lack of regard for his own life."

When Joanne asked about what should be done for James's disorders, Carol spoke without hesitation. "James Morrow is deeply disturbed, and my professional recommendation is that he should be committed to a mental health facility for immediate psychiatric treatment."

Joanne leaned in and told James that she wouldn't let him toss himself to the sharks that easily, adding that Carol was extremely popular among the public safety personnel. "A strong person to have on your side," Joanne said.

When the day of the verdict arrived, James sat in his cell, his foot bouncing on the floor and his jaw tight. He'd hardly slept, and his nerves were shot.

Television cameras and flashes assaulted him on his way into the courtroom. Members of the crowd yelled threats while others cheered. He heard several people yell, "Smuttynose Murderer." James's lawyer helped him put his suit coat on over his head.

In the courtroom, the jury appeared faceless. A woman stood and told the judge that the jury had found a verdict. The judge read the verdict and told the courtroom that James was found not guilty by reason of insanity. The judge then told James that he was sentenced to undergo treatment at a psychiatric facility where he would be eligible for an assessment hearing every ten years.

Joanne shook James's hand. "It's a good deal."

That was the last time James ever saw her.

A month later, Sam came to visit him in the facility. James had been leafing through the water-stained pages of Raymond Chandler's book *The Big Sleep* in the common area with the other patients. He needed to work on his socializing, or at least that was what his timid young blond psychiatrist (half the woman Carol had been) kept telling him. During patient free-time, he preferred to read on the couch. Besides, it wasn't as though he was a mute. He talked plenty, just not with anyone in that room.

James glanced up from his book and saw Sam standing in front of him, squinting. "Hardly recognized you."

"I recognize you." He dog-eared the page and placed the book on the cushion. Had it really been a month since he'd seen Sam? It seemed like years. After spending so much of his life overworking and trying to navigate lines through rapids, it had pained James to slow his life down to the stillness of a pond in the sterile halls of the psychiatric facility.

Sam pulled a chair over and sat in front of him. "You seem better."

James rubbed his fingers over his buzz cut. "My head's clearer."

"Making any new friends here?" Sam hooked his thumb toward the two guys playing air-hockey behind him.

The sounds of their puck clattering and the ticking ping of plastic ricocheting against plastic filled the common room most days. Ben and Ted were unlikely friends. Ben was a short wiry guy who talked as fast an auctioneer, and Ted was a linebacker in size who talked as slow as a child trying to read his first book. Sometimes Ted didn't bother talking at all, especially since half the time, Ben cut him down midsentence.

James leaned in close. "Do you have any news for me? The case?"

"Yeah, that's why I came."

Finally he would get his answer. He'd waited so long and thought maybe he'd never know. *Please, Sam, tell me who killed her.*

"You sure you can handle this? I don't want to set back your recovery."

"I can handle it, Sam. I need to know who killed her."

"Tucker Flynn." Sam let the name sink in for a moment. "One of the fishermen, guy named Tom Braxton, finally broke down and gave us the information for a slightly reduced sentence. Handed over a crowbar and ski mask with Tucker's DNA and fingerprints and showed us the boatyard where the attack happened."

James was speechless. It'd been Tucker all along. He'd come to James's house to help clean the puke off his shirt that fateful day and had gone with him to see Maya on the autopsy table. The others—the cops, Canadians, and the fishermen—had a part in it, but Tucker had been the one who actually killed her. Viciously beat Maya to death and lied to James on the boat that night...

"I hope that helps give you some closure." Sam wiped his palms on his jeans.

"It helps. Thanks, Sam."

When Sam left, he promised to come and visit again sometime. James wasn't going to hold his breath.

As free-time came to a close, he sauntered over to the line where they received meds. Today's nurse on duty was Meghan, a pop-tart kind of girl with strawberry hair, fresh out of community college. She smiled with that hawk-face of hers as she handed James his paper cup of pills.

He threw the cup back like a shot, jammed the pills into his gum line with his tongue, and pretended to swallow. He opened his mouth wide and left her with an enthusiastic "Thanks."

She smiled back. "You're welcome, James."

*Oh, Meghan, you're too sweet and trusting for this line of work.*

When he went back to his room, he spit the pills into the toilet while he peed. He hadn't been assigned another roommate since his last one got transferred to another hospital two weeks earlier. All the old man had done was sleep anyhow, and the times he *was* vertical, he groggily complained about how his meds made him tired. James didn't miss his company. In fact, the room seemed too crowded most days.

James lay on his twin bed with a sigh then turned on his side to face Maya. "Hey, babe."

"Hey, Jamesey." She offered him a generous smile and rested her hand on his chest.

# ACKNOWLEDGEMENTS

When it came to writing this book, I was helped by many brilliant people.

To my MFA crew, you guys continue to help me on a constant basis. Thanks for your many voices of reason.

A massive amount of appreciation goes to my writing mentors: Merle Drown, Katherine Towler, Craig Childs, and Robert Begiebing, who all helped me shape this landfill of words into a workable novel.

Big thanks to my beta reader and fellow writer Kelly Stone Gamble.

I want to thank my editors Michelle Rever and Cassie Cox, as well as the rest of the Red Adept Publishing staff. Thanks for taking a chance and publishing my book.

I want to thank my family and friends. You know who you are. You are all wonderful human beings. Here's a space for you to add your name to the book:

Thanks _____ , you're the best!